"I want to know where you got the song 'Gifted.'"

Callie O'Ryan felt Marc Raphael's surprise but refused to back away as his green eyes appraised her openly. She lifted her chin with defiance.

"'Gifted' will be on my new album," he hedged.

"There are laws against plagiarism!"

"Now, wait a minute—"

"No! You wait a minute!" Callie's blood raced hot through her temples, and she clenched her fists. "I wrote that song. I wrote it six years ago for my husband. I don't know how you got it, but *I* never gave it to you."

Marc carefully crossed his arms over his chest. "Are you accusing me of stealing, Mrs. O'Ryan?"

A Gift of Love

LURLENE McDANIEL

Serenade/Serenata
BOOKS
of the Zondervan Publishing House
Grand Rapids, Michigan

A Note from the Author:
I love to hear from my readers! You may correspond with me by writing:

Lurlene McDaniel
Author Relations
1415 Lake Drive, S.E.
Grand Rapids, MI 49506

A Gift of Love

Serenade/Serenata is an imprint of Zondervan Publishing House, 1415 Lake Drive, S.E., Grand Rapids, MI 49506.

ISBN 0-310-47591-0

Edited by Sandra L. Vander Zicht
Designed by Kim Koning

Printed in the United States of America

86 87 88 89 90 91 92 / 10 9 8 7 6 5 4 3 2 1

To all believers called to intercessory prayer,
to the "Miami years," and to my
Jewish friends. Shalom.

Prologue

THE ALLEY WAS COLD AND DARK. Kevin O'Ryan stamped the concrete pavement and rubbed his hands together to keep his limbs from going numb. He fingered his chin beneath his full red beard and allowed his hand to trail down his chest feeling for the wire taped under his flannel shirt and ski jacket. It was still in place.

To anyone peering into the darkened alley, Kevin looked like a street bum, huddled against the brick building for warmth and protection against the frigid November wind. But to the squad cars parked around the corner, he was the man in charge of the stake out. The detective was using himself as liaison and bait for a highly lucrative drug deal. If all went well tonight, they'd break up one of New York's biggest narcotic rings.

A scraping sound at the far end of the alley caused Kevin to crouch and reach instinctively for the gun usually nestled in the holster strapped around his shoulder. But it wasn't there. Tonight he was unarmed, a go-between for two drug kingpins. A cat darted between garbage cans, and Kevin straightened, forcing himself to take deep breaths and flex his tense, coiled muscles.

"I don't like the way this is going down," he mumbled into the microphone under his jacket. "My snitch should have been here a half hour ago. I'll give him fifteen more minutes, then I'm coming in." Kevin settled his arms across his massive chest and repositioned himself along the wall's stained, dank surface. Despite the cold, a fine film of perspiration formed across his muscular back. The alley reeked of stale garbage and years of gutter dirt. He wrinkled his nose in disgust.

In truth he didn't have the zeal for the undercover work anymore. He was tired of living on the cutting edge of life and death, worn out from ten years of mingling with society's lowest elements, fed up with the filth, the smells, the anguish. It was odd. He had once loved the job and thrived in the bizarre, sleazy world of the street people. When had it all changed?

When he'd met Callie. A half-smile softened the corners of his mouth as Kevin thought about his wife of ten months. *Callie* . . . with her thick strawberry-colored hair and dark brown, luminous eyes. How could one human being, with no more than a smile and the tilt of a turned-up nose, radically shake a man so firmly entrenched in his lifestyle as Kevin Patrick O'Ryan had been?

Callie had. Callie and the Lord. He'd met both of them on the same night, and his life had been forever changed. At thirty-five, Kevin O'Ryan knew he was a good detective. Street smart. Street tough. A survivor. But it wasn't until he'd met Jesus Christ that he'd known genuine salvation from the streets. And through that salvation, God's love. And that love had given him Callie. Yes . . . that's what she was to him. A gift. A gift granted by God's divine love.

And now with the baby coming . . . Kevin was glad that he'd made the decision to give up the street and put in for a desk assignment at the precinct. Tonight would be his final undercover job. This was his gift to Callie. The smile hovered on his mouth. Next week Callie'd be twenty-four. And part of his birthday present to her would be this permanent reassignment. This and the letter and the money. And of course, the yellow roses. He itched to give the letter to her, imagining her face as she read it. The money wouldn't mean half as much to her as the letter would.

He almost chuckled aloud, remembering her surreptitious searching of their apartment for her well-hidden birthday present. In the past two weeks, he'd observed her dusting closet shelves, sorting through the boxes and poking and peeking into every possible cranny she could think of—but even a detective's wife wouldn't think to look where he'd stored the letter for safekeeping. . . .

Another sound. Kevin jerked himself out of his reverie. "Is that you, Shilo?" Silence greeted his question. The air crackled with tension and a metallic taste formed in his mouth. Something was wrong. Every street instinct he had told him something was wrong. A shadow moved at the far end of the alley. Too big for a cat. A voice spat, "This is for you, cop!" And a flash of white erupted from the center of the dark shape.

A thudding blow hit Kevin in the chest, hurling him backward, hard against the wall. He clutched the front of his jacket and slid slowly to the cold ground. He struggled to rise, gasping for breath, felt a warm stickiness on his hand, and stopped struggling. Pain, like a searing fire spread down his chest, along his stomach, and across his back. From far away he heard running feet and the whine of sirens. Men shouted. Pistols cracked. The sounds grew faint as a frightening numbness snaked through him.

I'm dying! Dear Lord, I'm dying! For the briefest moment, Kevin felt regret. For Callie. For the baby. For the life they could never have. Then regret passed. This very night, Kevin O'Ryan knew he'd see the Lord, face to face. It made the pain more bearable. It made the leaving easier.

"O'Ryan! O'Ryan!" He heard men calling his name, but he couldn't answer them, didn't have the strength or the will to answer them. He fought against the darkness descending on him.

Callie! he thought. *Dear Lord, I give you back Callie. Protect her. Help . . . her . . . understand your . . . will. . . .* The darkness swooped lower. This time Kevin did not struggle. This time he rose to meet it, as on the wings of eagles.

chapter 1

"I TOLD YOU WE HAD FRONT-ROW SEATS, Callie. Now please, come sit down and try to enjoy yourself. It's going to be a good concert. Marc Raphael is one of the best." Farrell Hanson kept up a constant stream of talk as he led the reluctant Callie O'Ryan and his wife, Janette, through the scores of people milling around in the campus concert hall.

Callie forced herself to smile, tagging along behind her old friends Farrell and Janette, and admonishing herself every step of the way. *I shouldn't have come. Why oh why did I let Farrell talk me into coming?* The last place she wanted to be was in this giant auditorium amid all these eager young college kids waiting for a concert to begin—even if it were Marc Raphael singing.

"Here we are," Farrell interjected cheerfully. He pointed to three red cushioned seats, and Callie lowered herself into one. Janette settled next to her husband, opened the program, and laid it in Callie's hands.

"Look at this," Janette said. "We've got a half hour before the concert starts, but some of us always insist on being the first ones any place. . . ." She smiled as she shot her husband a sidelong glance. In this ability to communicate with a simple look, Callie felt the depth of their loving relationship. She clutched at the program, grateful. Trust Janette to know she was eager to have something to do with her hands.

"Now that you're here, aren't you glad you came?" Farrell's question caused Callie to lift her eyes to her friend's face. Farrell. Dear Farrell. He'd saved her sanity after Kevin's death. And her miscarriage.

She'd had such misgivings about coming to the concert. But the Hansons had insisted. Of course, they were right. She had to get out more often. But it was such an effort. Her heart wasn't into a social life yet. She sometimes wondered if it ever would be again. *Four years.* Four long years since that knock on her door in the middle of the night.

"I'm sorry to wake you, Mrs. O'Ryan. . . ."

"What's the matter? Has something happened to Kevin?"

"The bust went sour. Please, Mrs. O'Ryan. Let me help you to the sofa. Your condition . . . Sorry. So sorry . . ."

Four years. Every one of them stretched behind her like a long black ravine. It had taken a year for her to emerge from the dark, lonely pain of the double loss of Kevin and her baby. Then, when she realized she would have to begin rebuilding her life, the Hansons had contacted her. They went back a long way, to the time Callie was in college herself, when she'd been a part of Farrell's Campus Crusade ministry. It was Farrell who had secured her a position as music professor at the small Michigan college and Janette who had assimilated Callie into the surrounding community and made her feel a part of their family of three daughters. Without their love and support, Callie knew she would have never made it.

Janette leaned over to Farrell and tapped him on his arm. "Since we have a *few minutes* . . ." She emphasized the last two words. ". . . I think I'll call home and check on Melanie."

"Now, honey . . . ," Farrell started. "Terri and Jill are with her. She'll be fine."

Janette wrinkled her nose. "I know. But chicken-pox can lead to complications. I'd feel so much better if I called home."

Farrell released an exasperated sigh and let Janette pass. "Back in a moment, Callie."

"I'll make sure they hold the curtain for you," Callie called, smiling, sympathizing with her friend's dilemma. Six-year-old Melanie had been very sick, but she was on the mend, and Farrell had insisted his wife get out for the evening. Farrell had worked hard to get Marc Raphael to come to such a small campus for a concert. According to Farrell, Marc, appearing in nearby Detroit, had had to rearrange his busy schedule to perform tonight. Callie thought it a kind gesture on the musician's part, but judging from the growing size of the audience, it had also been a profitable move. Plus the popular singer's appearance would strengthen Farrell's campus ministry immensely.

"Now aren't you glad you came?" Farrell asked the question again, a beaming satisfied smile on his face.

"How could I resist coming?" Callie countered. "Your invitation was so persuasive. You and Janette practically hog-tied and dragged me here."

"Dragged you!" He pulled back in mock-horror. "I merely suggested that it was about time you got out of that stuffy little apartment and had some fun."

"Fun?" She arched her perfectly shaped eyebrow. "It's fun to mingle with kids, many of them *my* students, at a concert by a born-again former rock singer? No, Farrell, fun is sitting at home, munching popcorn, snuggling under an afghan, and listening to classical music, safe from the winds of March."

"Don't be such a recluse," he chided. "You're describing a form of vegetating, Callie—not fun. Besides, don't you know that it sets a good example for your students to see you out of your stuffy teacher's image and into 'what's happening now'?"

Callie giggled in spite of herself, but unconsciously she smoothed her lightweight navy wool skirt and tugged on the lapels of her cream-colored wool blazer. Her professor image was important to her. She worked hard to maintain credibility in her field of music. Farrell was almost forty. His hair contained a touch of distinguished gray at the temples. He looked the roles of instructor and minister. She, on the other hand, was often mistaken for a student.

Janette reappeared, slipped back into her seat with a flourish, and patted Farrell's hand. "Jill says Melanie's fine." Janette turned to Callie. "I told Jill to practice her piano tonight. You will come for her lesson Wednesday afternoon, won't you?"

"Would I miss a lesson with my favorite child prodigy . . . or a home-cooked meal by her mother?"

Janette warned, "Light fare this Wednesday. We have some of the students coming over for a Bible study. You will stay for it, won't you?"

Callie lowered her eyes self-consciously, fumbling with the forgotten program in her lap, at a loss for words. What could she tell Janette? How could she express her discontent, her soul-searching, her feelings of abandonment by God? Where was that wonderful faith she'd known in college? That wonderful, childlike faith that Farrell had helped spark when she was a freshman? *Vanished* . . . she mused. Vanished into that cold November night on a street of shadows, with an assassin's bullet. "Perhaps . . . ," Callie offered, her tone noncommittal.

Janette pointed to the program in Callie's hands, diffusing the tension between them. "Too bad the poor man's so ugly . . . ," she observed. Callie gazed down at the photograph of Marc Raphael on the cover, thankful for Janette's obvious attempt to lighten the mood. She thought Marc Raphael roughishly handsome with his longish dark hair, clear, piercing eyes, and square-cut jaw. High cheek bones, a strong, almost aquiline nose and a cleft in his chin gave his face a mysterious, quixotic look. Beneath his picture blazed the words: "Campus Crusade Presents Marc Raphael, The Lord's Troubadour."

"Yes . . . what a shame. . . . Would it shock you to know that I was once a groupie of Marc Raphael's? In the old days of course," Callie explained at Janette's questioning twinkle. "When I was still in high school and he was taking the rock music world by storm with that band of his, The Blades."

"High school?" Janette gasped with an exaggerated sigh. "Why, Farrell and I were old married folk with a five-year-old when you were in high school. And now you say you were chasing around after rock music stars? I'm shocked."

She feigned disbelief, her blue eyes growing large and animated.

"Believe it or not. My best friend, Rose Ann Taylor, and I saved our babysitting money for weeks in order to go hear Marc Raphael perform in concert in Madison Square Garden. I still remember the hysterical masses of screaming teenage girls. . . ." Her voice trailed, and she placed the back of her hand against her forehead, Sara Bernhart style, emphasizing the drama of the experience. "Of course, once I met Farrell and became a part of Campus Crusade, my jaded love of rock and roll diminished."

"But not your love of music," Farrell added.

"Never my love of music." That love had driven Callie to escape from her unhappy home life, work her way through college, and eventually get her degree in music.

Farrell leaned over and cocked his head. "Now that's a pretty sight."

"What?"

"The smile on your face. The light in your eyes. It reminds me of that lovely young girl who first joined my Campus Crusade group ten years ago."

Callie shrugged. Her smile faded, and she gave Farrell a wistful look. "It seems more like a hundred years ago. So much has happened. So much has changed. . . ."

Janette took her hand and squeezed it. "Life goes on, Callie." Her voice grew serious, earnest. "Somehow you've got to leave the past behind and start living again. It's time to stop mourning. Life goes on."

A taste of bitterness rose into her mouth. "I know life goes on," she said. "I wonder why. . . ."

I have no right to be bitter she admonished herself. Hadn't

God seen her through the darkness of those days after Kevin's death? Hadn't he been with her even after she'd miscarried? Hadn't he always sustained her? Watched over her? Helped her through the despair and the emptiness and the loneliness? Given her friends like the Hansons? A job? A new life in a new city? Yet she knew few twenty-eight-year-old widows. And she had yet to see light at the end of her tunnel of grief.

At that moment, the lights in the auditorium dimmed. People scurried for their seats. Conversation buzzed and dropped in expectation. Callie turned her attention to the stage, a scant fifteen feet in front of her. Giant speakers stood on either side and colored spotlights bounced off a red velvet curtain. She focused her attention on the evening ahead, telling herself that she would have a good time. Farrell and Janette were simply trying to be her friends. She had no right to make their evening unpleasant.

Callie watched the huge curtain rise and felt a flutter of anticipation in the pit of her stomach. All at once, she was glad she'd come. Marc Raphael had an interesting history. Callie recalled how his rejection of the rock music world and his confession of faith in Christ had shaken the secular music industry five years before. She remembered some of the ballyhoo and cutting skepticism in the tabloids at the time. Kevin had always liked Marc, talking about him as a kindred spirit on several occasions. She recalled the time she and Kevin had stood together in the grocery check-out line, and Kevin had picked up a notorious scandal sheet.

"It looks like Jesus has claimed another hard-core cynic."

"'Raphael Rejects Rock 'n' Roll for the Rock,'" Callie had read aloud. "I wonder—"

"If Christ can claim me, why not him?" Kevin's eyes had danced with amusement over her look of doubt.

"If he's giving up rock let him sing Christian," she'd shot back.

"It says that he will. He's dumping his band and going out on his own . . . as 'The Lord's Troubadour.' "

Callie had scoffed. "It's like day and night between those two worlds. After you've tasted the good life at the top, starting over can be very humbling."

The memory faded as Callie stared up at the stage. A microphone lay across a single chair set in center stage. A bright, white spotlight hit the tableau. From the stage wings a tall, square-shouldered man strode purposefully to the chair and into the spotlight, a classical guitar slung over his shoulder. Marc Raphael was dressed in black from head to foot. His legs were long, lean, his face was angular and intense. He moved with an easy animal grace, reminiscent of a panther.

Seeing him in the flesh caused a murmur to rustle through the crowd. Applause erupted as he fastened the microphone to a mike stand and lowered his lanky frame into the chair. In the spotlight his hair gleamed chestnut, full and straight, brushing the collar of his black turtleneck sweater.

Callie caught her breath. The stark simplicity of this setting contrasted sharply with his former one, when she'd seen him surrounded by his band members, a clutter of instruments, and swinging, dancing spotlights. Then, she'd been sitting hundreds of feet from the stage. Now, she felt like she was almost up there with him.

He plucked the strings of his guitar. The audience

waited. *He has us eating out of his hand* Callie thought with fascination. *It's as if he's all alone. As if he hasn't even noticed us yet.* She watched his long, masculine fingers trail over the strings, pulling melody from the heart of the instrument. Slowly, the musician looked up.

Callie leaned forward. Nothing had prepared her for the intense pure, clear green color of his eyes. It was the green of the first leaves of spring, the green of stained glass with sunlight behind it. "Hello. Greetings in the name of the Lord." His voice was soft, hinting of the rich baritone timbre that trademarked his songs. A slow smile started at the corners of his sensuous mouth and traveled the distance to his light-green eyes.

"Let me start with something old," he said. "Something I wrote on the night Christ saved me." He began singing then, lifting his voice and melding it into one with the guitar. Callie listened, mesmerized. She'd been a musician too long herself not to recognize extraordinary talent. How different he sounded from his days of heavy rock! Yet even then, he'd been heralded as an awesome talent. But now, here in the coolness of the auditorium, beneath the single spotlight, with only the guitar and his voice, Marc Raphael became bigger than life. His music, his songs had the power to touch and affect. Callie responded emotionally to the singular power of his gift.

He began a second song, scarcely giving the audience time to recover from the impact of the first one. His fingers strummed the guitar strings, trilling over a chorus that he matched with his voice.

"He's outstanding!" Janette's whispered comment startled Callie, snapping her out of the spell Marc Raphael was weaving around her.

"Yes," she murmured. "Outstanding."

His songs made her feel the presence of the Lord. Not like she felt when she was in church. It was as if she were sitting around a cooking fire with Jesus and listening to his parables.

Consider the lilies of the field,
How they grow
How they grow.
They toil not,
Neither do they spin,
They do not spin . . .
They do not spin . . .

Marc's melodious voice brought the scene alive for Callie. She envisioned the beautiful lilies fluttering and bowing in a summer wind, felt the depth of God's caring for his own. She was moved, touched by its simplicity. She longed to reacquaint herself with the God in Marc's song. *Kevin . . . if only . . .* Callie shook her head to chase away the ghosts of yesterday. How easy it was to slip into the past!

She willed herself to concentrate on Marc Raphael, feeling an odd kinship with him, a strange sense of bonding that reminded her of sun-kissed days with her husband. Somehow, the beauty of Marc's melodies, the richness of his voice brought Kevin closer.

He performed several more numbers, interweaving a selection of old gospel favorites with many of his own composition. He performed under a kaleidoscope of changing spotlights—red to yellow to orange. Every color underscored his choice of songs while his stark black apparel so drew attention to his face and hands that Callie found herself totally captured by the riveting power of his presence.

After a time, he stood, bowed to thunderous applause and waved to his audience. "I'm going to take a brief intermission," he told them, raking his straight, thick hair off his forehead with his fingers. "When I return, let's all praise the Lord together."

Callie watched him leave the stage as the houselights came up, feeling a strange disappointment that the first part of the concert was over so soon.

"What did I tell you?" Farrell exclaimed as the three of them rose to stretch cramped limbs. "Doesn't this beat popcorn and an afghan?"

She laughed, a bubble of genuine joy coming from within her. "I rescind my previous wish for a March night. You're right. This is far more enjoyable. Thank you, Farrell. Thank you for everything."

They wandered into the lobby where Janette and Callie threaded their way to the ladies room and joined a gaggle of buzzing females in front of a gleaming wall of fluorescent-lit mirrors. Callie frowned at her image. Her thick strawberry-colored hair needed combing to loosen the natural curls. Her face needed more blusher, and her lipstick had long since disappeared.

"Hello, Mrs. O'Ryan."

Callie turned to see the bright, young face of Sharon Lewis, one of her Music Theory students.

"Isn't he *wonderful!*" Sharon burbled. "I own every album he's ever made. And he's so good looking!"

Callie nodded. "Yes . . . he is wonderful. And he's also a brilliant technician." Sharon gave Callie a blank stare, and

Callie felt suddenly foolish and aloof from the enthusiastic girl. *Walls.* She thought. *Farrell says I'm always putting up walls between myself and the rest of the world.* Callie tried again to communicate, this time in a less formal manner. "Did you get the internship in that elementary school you wanted?"

"I sure did. Thanks for putting in a word for me with the dean."

"My pleasure. Anyone who wants to teach handicapped kids as bad as you do, should have the chance."

Sharon blushed and Callie found herself envying Sharon's youth, commitment and purpose. *I was like that once,* she thought ruefully. Once . . . when she'd been Kevin's wife . . . both of them so filled with plans and dreams. For each other. For the baby.

"The light just dimmed," Janette said in Callie's ear, snapping the mood of melancholy that had crept over her again. Callie hurried her make-up repairs and then followed Janette to their front row seats. The auditorium lights dimmed and the spotlight found Marc Raphael alone in the center of the stage.

As the spotlight widened around him, a piano stood etched out of the background shadows. Farrell leaned over and whispered, "He had this one flown in especially for tonight. The pianos in our music department wouldn't do."

Callie understood. As a musician, she knew about the special relationship an artist has with an instrument. Yet it must have cost a fortune to have it shipped in. "Who paid the tab?"

"Surprisingly, he did," Farrell said. "But then money's

no problem for a man like him. He made millions off the rock market. And from what I've read, he's not doing so bad in the Christian market either."

Not so bad . . . Callie thought, conscious of the packed auditorium. She focused on Marc's hands as they slid across the ivory keys of his gleaming black piano. Again she recognized his ability and years of formal training. She suppressed a smile. Kids thought it was so easy to play an instrument and warble a song and expect the money to roll in. Marc Raphael made it look so effortless that it's no wonder the misconception was maintained. She watched and listened, letting the magic of his music and voice ensnare her.

"You know," Marc began as his hands caressed the ivory keys, "there was a time when I sang different songs for a different crowd. . . . Wasn't I the fool?" A quiet laugh rippled through the audience. Marc's voice continued, light with a self-admonishing tone. "At twenty-three, I had everything the world had to offer. Everything. I spent four years on life's merry-go-round." Callie recalled splashy headlines about the Raphael legend—his parties, his women, his reckless lifestyle.

"You know what I discovered?" Marc asked. "I discovered that no matter how much I had, it still wasn't enough. It wasn't enough to fill up the void in my life. It wasn't enough to fill up the emptiness and the loneliness." His words drove into Callie like piercing arrows. *Loneliness.* She could write a dissertation on loneliness.

"I had everything except God," Marc said. The notes from the piano punctuated his monologue. "And do you know what else I discovered? I found out that without

Jesus Christ, I would always be lonely. And it wasn't enough just to be saved. I had to give Christ control of my life. Even if it meant giving up my singing career." He paused. "Fortunately, God had other plans . . . or I wouldn't be here tonight." The laughter raced through the audience again.

"Once I gave myself to him, he gave me a new singing career. Now, I sing a new song for a new King. God's timing is always perfect." Marc trailed over some minor keys, creating a sound of disharmony. "Sometimes it doesn't seem that way. Sometimes it seems like he's so far removed from us that we'll never touch him again. Like he's forgotten us . . . abandoned us. But he hasn't. If he cares about the birds of the air, how much more will he care for us?"

Callie's body went rigid, and she gripped the arms of her theater seat until her knuckles turned white. *Why is he saying those things? How does he know what I'm feeling?* She shook her head to clear it, grasping at her runaway emotions, feeling as if he had pulled out her innermost thoughts and exposed them to this crowd of people. She glanced around, certain that everybody was staring at her. But she only saw upturned faces, rapt attention on Marc. For a while his music had caused her to forget her hurts. But now he had brought them back with words of stunning clarity, words of stinging pain.

"I have a new song to share with you," Marc said suddenly, breaking the chain of tension he had created inside Callie. "I intend to include it on my next album. I like this one because it has a message of love, both for God and for a loved one. Friends," he paused dramatically. "I offer you . . . 'Gifted.'"

His fingers caressed the piano keys, and Callie blinked as a current of electricity shot through her. Perhaps she hadn't heard him correctly. Song titles . . . many were the same.

> With you I have the gift of love,
> With You I have love from above.
> I'm gifted . . .
> Gifted, by divine and human choice.

His voice sang clear and pure. Callie gasped, then reeled as if she been struck as Marc's resonant voice formed the words she knew so well, as Marc's hands played the tune she knew so completely. She blinked, struggling to shut out the sound of the song she never thought she'd hear again. The song she'd left buried in the tomb of yesterday. *My song!* A cry strangled in her throat. *That's my song for Kevin! Where? How did you get my song, Marc Raphael?*

chapter 2

"WHAT'S WRONG, CALLIE?" Janette's frantic whisper caused Callie to swivel in her seat.

"That song! Don't you recognize it? Am I going mad? That's the song I wrote for my wedding!"

For a few breathtaking moments, Janette said nothing. Then slowly, she nodded her head. "I only heard it once . . . at your wedding . . . but . . . but it does seem rather familiar."

Waves of nausea washed over Callie. She wanted to clamp her hands over her ears. She wanted to jump up and scream, "Stop!" She wanted to run. Instead, she sat, paralyzed with indecision, listening to the words, while the soft, haunting musical chords all but strangled her.

"What's the matter?" Farrell leaned over. Callie heard Janette tell him. "There's got to be a logical explanation . . . ," he countered.

But for Callie, there was only rage. Blind, hot, surging rage. Marc Raphael had stolen her song. Stolen and vilified the sacred, precious memory that was hers alone for Kevin. She felt Janette grip her hand. "It's all right, Callie. It'll be over in a minute." Her voice was soothing, like a mother's for a child.

Callie stared, dry-eyed, at the man in black, hating him, silently pleading with him to stop singing. To stop the torture he was inflicting on her soul. Mercifully, the music ended. The auditorium erupted in applause. Around her, people rose to their feet. Callie rose, too, and might have bolted onto the stage, except for Janette's restraining hand.

"Let's go to the lobby." Farrell's words were not a suggestion, but a command. Callie needed no urging. She sped up the aisle, past the throngs of applauding people, through the double doors and into the brightly lit lobby. She blinked, stopping to catch her breath, while Janette and Farrell came up on either side of her.

"He—he stole my song!" She almost choked on the words.

"Are you sure?" Farrell asked.

"Sure?" Callie exploded. "I know my own work! I wrote that song six years ago for Kevin. He liked it so much, he insisted it be sung at our wedding."

"But how could Raphael have gotten ahold of it?"

"I don't know. But I intend to find out." Callie's rage had turned to cold fury, a molten core surrounded by a glacial shell. "Help me find out, Farrell. After the concert, please take me to him."

Farrell's voice grew conciliatory. "Callie, perhaps if you waited . . . contacted a lawyer . . ."

She whirled. "I want to see him tonight! If you won't help me, then I'll march up onto that stage right now and cause a scene he won't soon forget."

Janette reached around Callie's shoulders. "That won't be necessary. I'm sure Farrell will get you in to see Mr. Raphael after the concert." Callie saw her flash her husband a pleading glance.

"Of course I will. But it might be a long wait."

"I've got all night."

She waited, pacing in the lobby, simmering in the juices of her anger. *Kevin! If only you were here!* He would have helped her deal with Marc Raphael. Kevin would have known what to do. *Perhaps if he'd never met me, he'd be alive still.* She'd changed him somehow. Some subtle way that had made him less eager for the work he did. Less sharp. More vulnerable.

Callie paused in front of a large concert poster of Marc. She scanned his perfectly chiseled face, seeing no hint of duplicity in his eyes. No trace of the nature that would cause him to steal a song and claim it as his own. Deceptions. The world was filled with deceptions. And injustices.

It seemed like an eternity before the audience surged through the doors of the auditorium, into the lobby. Callie watched them, heard them laughing, praising the performance. Bitterness rose like quinine in her mouth. The crowds thinned. At last Farrell took her arm. "Are you ready?"

She stepped in front of him, back inside the concert hall, now blazing with light. The red seats looked forlorn and deserted. The floor was littered with traces of the spectators: popcorn boxes, cola cups, napkins, and abandoned programs. Stagehands cleared the stage, wrapping cords, and breaking down the simple set. Two men shoved the baby grand into the wings, toward a massive double door that opened into the raw March night. A truck bed yawned to receive the huge instrument.

"The dressing rooms are back this way. . . ." Farrell picked his way through the maze of equipment. Callie hesitated, less sure of the path. She forced herself to breathe deeply, swearing she'd confront Marc Raphael without tears and hysterics.

A security guard materialized and blocked their way. "Can I help you?"

"It's Farrell Hanson, Joe. I need to see Mr. Raphael."

The guard smiled and pointed to an inconspicuous door. "He's alone now. The young man from the campus newspaper just left."

Callie's heart pounded, but her intent had not dulled. Farrell rapped on the door, and a voice answered, "Come in." The three of them walked into the small dressing room, Farrell, then Callie and Janette.

Marc Raphael sat on a worn sofa, his long legs spread in front of him, his arms draped across the back, in an attitude of total exhaustion. He was still dressed in black. He rose, hesitant at first. Then, recognizing Farrell, he offered his hand, a smile lighting up his marvelous green eyes.

Callie measured him, awed in spite of herself over his instant charisma. "Farrell!" Marc's voice greeted, genuinely surprised. "I'm glad you came backstage. Thank you for inviting me here. The audience was tremendous, and it was a blessing for me to perform for them."

Callie saw Farrell drop his gaze. "Uh—thank you, Mr. Raphael. . . ." He cleared his throat. "Uh—I have someone here . . ."

She stepped boldly forward, shouldering his embarrassment, relieving him of his awkward position. "My name is Callie O'Ryan, Mr. Raphael." She sounded abrupt, curt. She didn't care. "I want to know where you got the song 'Gifted.' "

She felt Marc's surprise but refused to back away as his green eyes appraised her openly. She lifted her chin with defiance.

"'Gifted' will be on my new album."

"There are laws against plagiarism!"

"Now wait a minute—"

"No! You wait a minute!" Callie's blood raced hot through her temples, and she clenched her fists. "I wrote that song. I wrote it six years ago for my husband. I don't know how you got it, but I never gave it to you."

Marc carefully crossed his arms over his chest. "Are you accusing me of stealing, Mrs. O'Ryan?"

"That's exactly what I'm accusing you of, Mr. Raphael."

"And where is your husband? Can he corroborate your story?"

Color drained from her face, leaving it pinched and white. "Kevin . . . my husband's dead. He was shot to death four years ago." She heard her voice quaver, but she swallowed and forced the lump down in her throat.

"Mrs. O'Ryan . . ." Marc's tone became gentle, beguiling. "I'm sorry about your husband. But I did not steal your song."

"Then where did you get it?" Tears threatened again as her anguish bubbled to the surface.

Farrell interrupted. "Callie . . . Mr. Raphael . . . please." He turned first to Marc. "Look . . . this has been a rough four years for Callie. Hearing that song tonight was too much. She's telling you the truth. It was sung at her wedding. My wife and I were both there. We heard it."

"Now you're accusing me of stealing too?" Marc raked his long fingers through his thick dark hair. "Listen, all of you. I write most everything I sing. Occasionally, I buy songs from outside vendors. But they're always professional writers—never amateurs. I did not steal your song, Mrs. O'Ryan."

Callie shook with rage. "Are you calling me a liar? I know what I wrote, 'Gifted' is *my* song." Callie paced the length of the stuffy, cramped room liked a caged tigress. Finally she spun to confront him. "It's mine and I can prove it!"

He was leaning against the counter in front of the dressing room mirror. Round, bright light bulbs blazed from the perimeters of the mirror. From where she stood, Callie could see him front and back, his broad square shoulders reflected in the glass. "How do you intend to back up your claim?" His voice turned challenging.

Callie glared at him. His eyes held an open declaration of war. Momentarily, she fought confusion, casting about for some proof to endorse her claim. *The tape!* Of course . . . the tape of the wedding ceremony. She had it somewhere. But where?

"Proof? You want proof? I can give you that. Oh, it may take a few days, but I can get it."

Marc measured her. "Then I suggest you get it," he said quietly. "And it had better be irrefutable."

She saw her reflection in the mirror give him a wicked, triumphant grin. "I have the voice of a dead man on an audio cassette, complete with the song. Will that be proof enough?"

Marc arched his eyebrow at her. "I'll be waiting."

Callie took a deep, shuddering breath and asked the wide-eyed Janette, "Can we go now?" She moistened her parched lips with the tip of her tongue and crossed to the door, where she paused. "Mr. Raphael . . ." Callie turned toward him. He still leaned against the counter, his body seemingly relaxed. But a veil had dropped over his eyes. She couldn't read his thoughts. "What is the status of the album you spoke about tonight?"

"I've selected it to be the lead number on the album I plan to cut in the fall."

"May I suggest that you delay your plans. I intend to obtain an injunction against your unauthorized use of 'Gifted.' It's my song. You stole it. And I can prove it. My lawyers will be in touch." Her hand closed over the hard, cold doorknob.

"Mrs. O'Ryan." She stiffened her back, but refused to turn again to meet his eyes. "I do not steal. I didn't when I was in the rock music profession. And I don't now that I'm in the kingdom of God. Don't think that you can walk in and out of my life, flinging false accusations at me and hiring attorneys to do your work for you. We will meet again, Mrs. O'Ryan. You can count on it."

Callie leaned against the car seat, feeling deflated, drained. Her head throbbed. The quiet drone of the engine soothed her, while the warmth of the heater thawed her icy feet and hands.

"Are you all right?" Janette asked.

Callie offered her friend a wan smile as the woman glanced into the back seat at her. "No," she confessed. "But I will be." Streetlights flashed through the windows in a rhythmic pattern that Callie found oddly comforting. She closed her eyes and allowed the light to splash over and over across her lids. "Thank you for supporting me in that dressing room."

"We're with you all the way." Farrell spoke with determined assurance.

"Oh, Callie," Janette moaned. "How I wish you didn't have to go through all that pain tonight. It's all such a mystery. . . ."

"He won't get away with it." She wished she could sound more forceful, but the fight had gone out of her. Now she was tired. So tired. The song ran through her head. Not the remembered version that she'd often played and sang for Kevin, but Marc's version, haunting, ethereal. She opened one eye and peered into the outer darkness. "This isn't the way to my apartment."

"You're coming home with us," Farrell told her.

"Oh, but I can't—"

"Nonsense," Janette interjected. "You're totally drained. I want you home with us. I know you'll go to bed in my guest room. You may not in your apartment."

"But I have so much to do. . . ."

"It'll keep. Tomorrow's Friday. I know for a fact that you don't have a class until one o'clock. Get a good night's sleep, get up in the morning, and I'll fix you breakfast, then I'll take you home. Promise. Besides," Janette added hastily, "the girls will be delighted to get up in the morning and see Aunt Callie. Especially, Melanie. You know how she adores you."

Callie tried to form words of protest. But she couldn't. The truth was she didn't want to return to her cold, lonely apartment. Janette was right. At home, she would not sleep. She would pace the floor, searching for the strength to go through the boxes.

A bitter smile twisted her mouth in the dark as she thought about the boxes. It was all that remained of Kevin O'Ryan's thirty-five years on earth. Friends, wives of other policemen, had come in and packed them up for her, storing away all the mementos and memorabilia of his life and their brief marriage. In the four years since his death, she'd never found the strength to go through them. Now, she had to. She had to find the tape that would prove her claim on the song, "Gifted."

Callie sighed. "I won't argue with you. Take me home with you and tuck me in. I guess you're right. Tomorrow is soon enough to get started."

"Of course, it is." Janette said soothingly. "After some sleep, some food, and in the clear light of day, you'll feel much better."

Callie closed her eyes again. She doubted it. She tried to pray, but couldn't. *Where are you, God? Why don't you answer me? Why don't you care?* Aloud, she asked, "You know what the ironic part is?"

Neither Janette nor Farrell spoke. "I used to write songs for Marc Raphael. That's right. When I was a kid and he was on top of the music world with his band. I used to sit for hours and make up songs on the piano at home. Of course, in my imagination he always sang them, and they all became big hits.

"When I went to his concert with Rose Ann, I took some of my songs with me. I was so sure I could get backstage, thrust them into his hands, and have him fall all over himself accepting. But once the concert was over, I couldn't have gotten backstage with a Mack truck. . . ." Callie rubbed her hand across her eyes. "Funny . . . I hadn't thought about that in years. . . ."

"God works in mysterious ways . . . ," Janette began.

"Spare me the platitudes," Callie snapped alert, her voice rising in pitch. "Five years ago I had everything that I ever wanted. It makes no sense to me that God would give me so much, only to snatch it away so completely."

Janette sighed. "I don't pretend to understand it. But I do know that he still cares about you. And I believe that this episode with the song is not to dredge up the past, but to somehow pave the way for the future."

Callie gave her a baleful look. "I have no future, Janette. But I do have a song that was meant for Kevin. And I intend to keep it. No matter what."

Marc Raphael sat alone in his luxurious hotel suite. The room was so dimly lit that he could see his reflection in the bank of glass windows that overlooked the Detroit River and the twinkling lights of Windsor, Canada, far below. Since it took him hours to come down from the high of a public performance, he still felt wound up, tight and euphoric from the concert. He shook his head of thick, dark hair, damp from the shower, and tried to assimilate the events of the evening. No matter how hard he tried, he couldn't get that woman out of his mind.

Haunted. That's how she had looked. Haunted and lonely. And scared. It might not have bothered him so much except that he'd seen the look before . . . seen it in his own eyes, peering back from a mirror over five years before. The night Vince had shouted, "*Hey! Look at me! I'm Superman.*" Marc shut his eyes, struggling to wipe out the image of his one-time band member. The woman—Callie O'Ryan—had brought it back. The old days, his other life . . .

He purged his thoughts with a quick prayer and turned his attention to the more practical aspects of the dilemma she presented. *The song. What am I'm going to do about the song?* He knew he had to call Alex. As his manager and friend, Alex might know where to start to untangle the mess. And what to do about his future record album. He wanted to use the song—had planned the theme of the entire record around it. Yet until the matter of ownership was cleared up, his hands were tied.

Marc sighed, picked up the phone and called Nashville. After six rings, a sleepy voice mumbled, "Hello?"

"Alex, it's Marc."

Silence, then, "If this is a social call . . ."

"Business."

"It couldn't wait? Good grief. According to my watch, Mickey's little hand is on the two . . ."

"In Detroit, Mickey's little hand is on the three," Marc told him gently. "You know I wouldn't have called unless I needed to."

Marc heard Alex fumble with the receiver, envisioning him groping for his glasses on his nightstand. He heard a muffled, "What is it?" as Alex's wife awoke. After assurances, Alex said in a less sleepy voice, "I'm awake. What's up?"

"I've got problems." Quickly, Marc told Alex about Callie, the song, and the threatened lawsuit. A prolonged silence followed. Marc pictured his friend's face, intense, serious.

"Where *did* you get the song?"

Marc shook his head. "I can't remember the circumstances too clearly. I do remember finding it in an old file drawer six months ago. Because it was there, I just assumed I owned it. I guess I bought it years ago and filed it away. But I don't remember for sure."

"Well, if you bought it, surely the seller signed a contract."

"My life was pretty crazy five years ago," Marc reminded Alex. "I'd just announced my retirement, confessed my new-found faith, left the band. The press was all over me. I had fifty lawsuits for breach of contracts. . . . You know how it was."

Alex chuckled. "That's when we met. It took me months to straighten out the mess."

"Anyway, I think I remember receiving the song in the mail."

"You bought a song by mail?" Alex sounded incredulous. "Marc, you buy magazines by mail. Or clothes. You don't buy songs."

A wry smile quirked Marc's mouth. "I liked it."

"Well, if you didn't get a contract, how did you pay for it?"

"Maybe by check."

Alex perked audibly. "That's our first glimmer of hope. If the seller cashed the check, then we at least have some legal grounds for ownership."

"Five years is a long time . . ."

"I'll call your CPA first thing in the morning. He should have your old tax records. Don't panic yet. Let me check this out."

Marc waited, almost hearing the wheels turning in Alex's head. "There's one more thing."

"Can my heart stand 'one more thing'?"

"The woman . . . the one who claims the song is hers. I want to know more about her."

"Why?"

"She's hurting, Alex."

Alex groaned. "Another potential project, Marc?" His tone reflected old arguments from their past.

"Look, music is my ministry. The money I make from it goes to God's work—wherever it is. I promised him that a long time ago."

"You already support more people, projects, and organizations than the United Way," Alex grumbled.

Marc laughed. "Old friend, I've often said I'd trade the money for more time to minister."

Alex sighed heavily. "All right. What's the woman's name?"

"Callie O'Ryan. She's involved with Farrell Hanson and his college campus ministry somehow."

"How long will you be in Detroit?"

"I have another concert at Cobo Hall a week from tomorrow to kick off my Midwest tour. I had intended to fly back to Nashville between engagements. But now I think I'll stay on until I hear from Callie O'Ryan or her lawyers."

"Maybe I can give you something to fight them with. Let me get back to you after I talk with your CPA and your attorneys." Alex paused, then added, "Just a word of advice, Marc. Don't let this woman get to you. She could be pulling a scam, you know. I assume she's not ugly."

Marc chuckled, amused at his friend's insightful warning. "Strawberry blond with big brown eyes. She's not hard on the eyes. Don't worry. I won't let her bedazzle me."

They said their good-bys and Marc recradled the phone, a smile still playing on his mouth. No. Callie O'Ryan was most definitely not ugly. Momentarily, he wondered what her hair would feel like in his fingers. Or her cheek against his palm. Marc shook his head, dismissing the course his thoughts had taken. Alex was right. He couldn't let her get under his skin.

He stood, stretched, finally feeling wound down from the intensity of his performance. Absently, he crossed the carpet in bare feet, paused in front of his piano and picked out a few chords from the melody of "Gifted." The music stirred him. He'd known it was good the first time he read it and played it; he was smart enough about the industry to recognize a song with hit potential. Callie O'Ryan was no novice to music. Whoever she was, she was well trained in her discipline. He sang softly, ". . . I'm gifted, Gifted by divine and human choice."

This Kevin had been loved. Marc could sense it in the poignancy of the song's words and the beauty of the melody. "He's dead . . . ," she had said. Again, Marc remembered the pain in her eyes when she had told him. Her song was her monument to that love, and Marc realized that when he had sung it publicly, he had desecrated the monument and become her enemy.

Marc raked his hand through his hair and quickly lowered the lid over the row of ivory and black keys, striving to put the song and the woman out of his mind. He went to bed and lay wide awake in the darkness, unable to do either.

chapter 3

"BACON AND EGGS SOUND OKAY TO YOU?" Janette called from where she stood in front of the stove, turning bacon with a long-handled fork. Callie raised her eyes over the rim of her coffee cup as the rich aroma of cooking food and perked coffee permeated the butter yellow kitchen.

"Sounds wonderful," she answered, arching her back, easing the tightness across her shoulders, and pulling Janette's borrowed terry bathrobe closer to her lithe body.

"I told you things would be better after a night's sleep."

Things weren't better, but Callie swore to pretend they were. The kitchen suddenly erupted into a cacophony of noise and motion as Melanie, Jill, and Herman, their English sheepdog, bounded through the doorway.

"Aunt Callie!" Melanie flung herself into Callie's welcoming arms. Callie smoothed the child's long blond hair and examined her remaining chicken-pox marks. "You look about ready to face the world again. How do you feel?"

Melanie wrinkled her nose and made a face. "Scabbie."

"Yeah, she's getting sassy, so I know she's getting well," Jill interjected with a roll of her eyes.

"I am not!"

"Girls . . . girls . . . please . . ." Janette padded to the table and set down platters of eggs and bacon. "Start eating. Your father will be wanting to leave in ten minutes. Where's Terri?"

"Primping," Jill offered. "She's crazy for Jimmy Donaldson, and it takes her twice as long to get dressed in the morning."

Farrell hustled into the kitchen, his dress shirt half buttoned. He kissed his wife soundly and sat at the table. "Morning!"

Callie, feeling a twinge of sorrow over their familial contentment, took a sip of scalding coffee and turned her attention back to Melanie. "How's school? Are you caught up on your work?"

"Nothing else to do," the child grumbled. "Besides, Mrs. Brewster says I have to practice my penmanship. I make sloppy alphabets. I hate practicing."

"You can practice on me," Callie volunteered. "Write me letters."

"Can I?"

"Any time you want."

"Herman!" Janette's voice broke shrilly. "Get out of the bacon! Jill . . . put the dog outside. And I mean now!"

"Come on, girls," Farrell said impatiently glancing at his watch. "Let's get a move on. Where's Terri?"

Thirteen-year-old Terri rushed into the kitchen, head down, mumbling, "I'll wait for you in the car, Dad."

"Wait a minute!" Farrell reached out and halted her, mid-flight. "Let me see your face."

"Oh, Daddy . . ."

He scanned her petite features. "Wash off the eye shadow, back off on the blusher, and forget the lipstick."

"But, Daddy!" She wailed. "I'll look like a ghost! All the other girls . . ."

Farrell shook his head in bemused tolerance. "But you're not like all the other girls. Now go wash your face."

Terri stomped out of the kitchen in a huff, yet Callie admired Farrell's firm but loving handling of his oldest girl. She wondered, fleetingly, what kind of mother she would have been.

Once Farrell and his daughters had left, and Melanie had returned to her bedroom, Janette sank into a kitchen chair and poured herself a fresh cup of coffee. "Are they gone?" She asked, peeking through one eyelid.

Callie chuckled. "Like a swarm of locust."

Janette hunched toward her. "Then let's talk. Any more thoughts about last night?"

"I still intend to find that tape of my wedding ceremony and stop Marc Raphael from using my song."

"Do you have any idea how he might have gotten it in the first place?"

"Can't even venture a guess." Callie set her cup down on the glossy pine table top. "Do you know what's really crazy? No one would have been more pleased to have Marc Raphael singing that song than Kevin."

"Really?"

"Kevin liked Raphael. He avidly followed his career once Marc became a Christian. I think Kevin empathized with him. It wasn't easy on him at the precinct house when he started following the Lord . . . dealing with the people he had to deal with . . . pimps, prostitutes, drug addicts—even his co-workers gave him a hard time.

"But when he read about Marc Raphael giving up all that fame and fortune to walk the same path—well, Kevin told me once that Raphael was what the rich young ruler could have become if he had been willing to give up his possessions when Jesus asked him to."

Janette reached over and took Callie's hand. "Are you sure you want to go through this fight?"

Callie stiffened. "It's not merely the song." She dropped her gaze. "It's just that it's *mine*. Mine and Kevin's. I want to keep it for us."

"It's too beautiful to keep locked away," Janette told her gently. "Maybe you can work something out with Mr. Raphael . . ."

"No!" Callie cut her friend off curtly. She stood, determined to substantiate her claim. The sooner, the better. "I really would appreciate it if you'd take me home now. I need to prepare for class." *And I need to start on those boxes,* she finished to herself. By tonight she'd be able to prove "Gifted" was hers and stop Marc Raphael from singing it, from claiming it as his own.

Callie sat on the edge of her cream-colored sofa, staring at the two cardboard boxes perched on her coffee table. She'd managed to get them down off the shelf in her bedroom before class, but all she'd done was sit and stare at them all afternoon long.

"Just open them up," she said aloud, startling herself with the sound of her own voice. She went to her stereo and turned on an album of classical music. The quiet strings of a symphony calmed her. Outside, darkness gathered, so she turned on more lamps to chase away the shadows. But the boxes beckoned unrelentingly. Her heart hammered as she returned, settled on the sofa and carefully pulled back the flaps on the smaller one.

Inside, she discovered Kevin's baseball hat. She ran her hand over the sweat-stained crown, tracing the word "Royals" with her fingernail. He'd been first baseman on the precinct softball team. Next, she found framed commendations from the New York Police Department along with a medal and his shield. She allowed the badge to catch the lamplight and reflect sparks of silver into her eyes. Callie sniffed, clenched her fist, and shoved the shield aside.

She found mementoes from his desk, an old chess set he'd bought at an antique shop once, a dog-eared Bible. She flipped the pages, a lump in her throat as she scanned his various notations. She remembered how they'd met, at a Crusade for Christ rally. He'd been sent to watch the crowd for drugs . . . dressed like one of the college students. She'd been incensed, indignant . . . blasting him with an angry tirade that had only caused his blue eyes to twinkle.

"It's my job." His broad shoulders shrugged.

"Indeed! Well, these are Christians, Mr. O'Ryan. There's nothing like that going on here!"

Farrell had preached, and Kevin had come back the next night and the night after that. Then on the last night of the rally, he'd gone to the front when Farrell had asked for a commitment to Christ. Open-mouthed, Callie had gaped as the big, tough red-haired cop had knelt for prayer. When he'd come back up the aisle, he'd hugged her, impulsively, picking her up off the ground and swinging her around.

"I'm very pleased for you . . . ," she stammered.

"Pleased?" he boomed. "Be pleased for both of us, pretty Callie. Because you're the woman I'm going to marry!"

Callie shook her head, the smile hovering on her lips as she recalled that night so long ago. He'd been right. She had married him. *And then I lost him. . . .*

"Stop it!" Callie demanded of herself, pushing the memories away. "Just find the cassette and stop living in the past." Her fingers dug down into the box with renewed determination.

She pulled out a framed photograph of their wedding day, the picture they'd kept on the dresser near their bed. Her heart thudded, and she tenderly swept the dust off the surface of the glass. Figures, frozen in time, smiled out at her. Kevin was dressed in a formal black tuxedo. His hair gleamed red in the candlelight; his beard was clipped and trimmed. She stood next to him, holding a bouquet of yellow roses, her white gown a shimmering chrysalis that swirled around her feet. Her eyelet veil rose from a headpiece of seed pearls and trailed over the red carpet of the church altar. From overhead, a stained-glass window cast rainbow patterns on their shoulders.

Callie caught her breath, remembering . . . as flushing tenderness spread through her insides. How gentle he'd been with her that night. Leading her, carefully, lovingly, down the path of physical union to completeness . . . to oneness. *"For better, for worse, in sickness and health . . . till death do us part . . ."*

She clasped the photograph to her breast and closed her eyes. Her arms ached to hold him. Her body longed to feel his next to hers, hard and muscled. She trembled, recalling the flutter of his bearded mouth on her skin. She blinked, wide-eyed, forcing away the warmth that had crept over her. The softness was gone. Instead, there was only the hard, cool, unyielding surface of the glass against her body.

She almost tossed the picture aside, except something caught her eye. A ripple in the photograph's smooth surface. Callie squinted and drew the framed picture under a lamp for closer scrutiny. *I don't remember it being bumpy. . . .* Yet it was. A definite lump distorted the photo in its center. Quickly, she turned it over and slid the backing off. Beneath the cardboard backing, she found a card.

Callie's hands trembled as she turned it over. On its cover was an Impressionist painting of a vase of summer flowers. Inside was the printed message: "Happy Birthday, I love you" and a handwritten note. There was also a folded piece of stationery. Gingerly, her head feeling light, Callie unfolded the paper. It contained a typed message on letterhead marked "Raphael." And there was something else too. Stunned, she watched while five crisp, one hundred dollar bills fluttered noiselessly to the floor.

Marc paced the carpeted suite, pausing in front of the windows to pull back the drapes and let the dazzling spring sunlight stream into the room. A cloudless azure sky balanced the bright ball of the sun while below a barge floated like a toy in the brown-colored water of the river. But then from sixty stories high, the entire world looked toylike to him. Marc stared out pensively for a few moments, shrugged the tension off from between his shoulders, and returned to his pacing.

In a little while, Callie O'Ryan would be coming up to his suite here in the glass tower of Detroit's Renaissance Center. He probably shouldn't be seeing her alone, without his attorney, but he hadn't been too rational about the woman ever since he'd first met her the week before.

Over the phone, her voice had been soft, breathy, hesitant. "May I please see you, Mr. Raphael. Please. It—it's very important."

He'd told her to come, doing what he never did, giving out his room number and notifying the desk to allow her entry onto the special elevators that led to this exclusive wing of the hotel. He crossed the pale peach-colored carpet to the glass-topped table and flipped open the folder that held Alex's findings on Callie, as well as the photostat of a cancelled check. He frowned at the endorsement. "Kevin P. O'Ryan." The proof was irrefutable. For some reason, Callie's husband had sold the song "Gifted" to Marc four years before. He didn't want to hurt Callie with the information, but he was, after all, the rightful owner of the song.

Room service interrupted his thoughts. He let the waiter pull the cart in front of the table, tipping him generously for the silver carafe of coffee, an assortment of cheese and fruit, and a tray of petits fours. After the waiter left, Marc shoved the folder into a drawer, wrestling with his conscience. He didn't want to wound her, didn't want to see that haunted look in her eyes again. But he had a lot at stake.

According to the brief dossier, she taught music at the college, having arrived from New York City a year after her husband's death. He knew Farrell had gotten her the job.

He knew that she had a few private piano students to supplement her teacher's income. He knew she had no other life than her job and her friendship with the Hansons. It seemed a Spartan existence for one so young and beautiful. When a knock sounded on his door, Marc shoved the file folder between the sofa cushions.

As the door opened, Callie attempted to smile. Her knees shook, feeling rubbery. She hoped she could control the quiver in her voice. It wasn't going to be easy to beg this man's forgiveness. Especially not after all the hot angry words she had flung at him. She hoped the dress she'd chosen—after an hour's deliberation—was suitable. She adjusted the cowl collar on the pale blue lightweight jersey and extended her hand, all the while gazing into the clear depths of his brilliant green eyes.

Her insides went mushy as he took her hand and said, "Come in. I've been expecting you." Simply knowing she was in the presence of a man she had once idolized, almost made her turn and bolt. *Marc Raphael.* Suddenly, she found herself tongue-tied like a silly school girl.

"It's good to see you again, Callie." He took her hand and led her into the room. His palm was warm and his smile familiar. She'd seen it hundreds of times on album covers and posters, but now it was real. And it shone on her, lighting the way for her to finally speak. "Thank you for seeing me, Mr. Raphael."

"Marc," he said. "Sit down. Let me pour you some coffee."

She complied, scanning the luxurious suite, beautifully accented in shades of peach and forest green. She took the coffee, but doubted she'd be able to swallow it. *How do I begin?* She'd rehearsed a hundred scenarios, but now her mind went blank. "I owe you an apology. . . ." She allowed her hands to clasp in her lap, locking her fingers together in taunt expectation.

"How so?" He lifted one dark eyebrow, quizzically.

"Well . . . it seems . . . that is . . . you really do own 'Gifted.'" She felt her heart pounding against her rib cage.

"Do I?"

"Yes. Can I start at the beginning?" He flashed her an encouraging smile and motioned with his head for her to continue. "My husband was a policeman. He was also a Christian. He was on his last undercover assignment and something went wrong. He . . . he was killed." She dropped her gaze, struggling to regain her composure. "That all happened four years ago—a week before my birthday."

Marc lifted his eyebrow again. "I had written that song for him when we were still dating. It was especially personal, private. But it was his. I–I guess he wanted to surprise me. He sent it to you without telling me. You bought it. I–I found the money. . . ." She paused for a moment, twisting her empty ring finger.

"Friends packed up Kevin's belongings for me . . . including his intended birthday gift. When I went through his old things last week, I found a birthday card and a note from him. In it, he explained how he had sent the song off . . . never dreaming you'd actually buy it. I mean a star like yourself . . ." Her words trailed, and she squirmed under his soft gaze.

"How do you feel about it now?"

"Ashamed of the way I acted in your dressing room. I'm very sorry. I–I should never have said those things to you—accused you unjustly." The color rose in her cheeks, and she found it impossible to look directly into his eyes. "I've had a week to think about it. Having you sing the song was what Kevin wanted." She lifted her shoulders in a gesture of submissive understanding, not resignation. "I'm honored that you're singing it. I know Kevin would be too."

"You write beautiful songs, Callie."

She blushed, more from remembered girlhood fantasies than his praise. She'd heard him tell her that many times in her dreams. And now that he was actually saying it . . . What an odd twist of events to have brought her to this place in time!

Callie untangled her fingers, flexing them, and gave Marc a tentative smile. "I guess that's what I came to say. I'm so sorry I lambasted you the way I did. Forgive me."

"I understand. It must have been a shock . . . hearing me sing a song you'd written without knowing how I'd gotten it."

Callie rose. "Thank you for your time . . . and your understanding." She'd said her piece and felt an urgency about leaving. She'd intruded enough into his life already. He rose next to her. Even in her heels, she barely reached to his chin. His V-neck burgundy cashmere sweater allowed the dark mat of his chest hair to show. She took a step backward.

"Callie . . ." He stopped her, touching her arm. "Let's start all over again. I'd like to do something for you to make up for any hurt I've caused."

"Oh no, that's not necessary. You've already been too kind. . . ."

Marc didn't want her to go, feeling strangely compelled to know her better, to strip off her veneer of unhappiness and make her laugh. "I've been intending all week to drive across the border into Canada, but so far I've never had the time. Today I do. Would you come with me?"

"Oh . . . I–I don't know . . ."

"Do you have other plans?" Her eyes were round, fawn-colored. He almost stroked her hair. From within, Alex's voice chided, *"You can't heal every hurt in the world, Marc. Leave some things to heaven."*

"No."

"Then come with me. We'll do some sightseeing in Windsor, have supper in a special French restaurant I've heard about. It would be relaxing for me, but not much fun alone."

Something leaped up within Callie. Some feminine need to be pampered, escorted, admired by this attractive man. The way he looked at her made her feel pretty. How long had it been since she'd felt these sensations? How long since she'd felt these stirrings? "I guess it wouldn't be much fun alone." Her smile broke, radiant. "I'd love to come. Do you know I've lived in Michigan for almost four years, and I've never been across the border?"

"I can remedy that." He crossed to a closet and pulled out a brown leather jacket and a brown felt fedora. The hat made him look both rakish and debonair. He offered her his arm. "Shall we?"

She locked her elbow with his and tilted her chin upward. The darkness that had hung on her for the previous week evaporated as the sunlight from the windows poured over her and the warmth of his presence engulfed her.

Windsor, Canada, was quaint and picturesque. But a stone's throw from Detroit, its atmosphere was decidedly British, genteel and unhurried. The drive across the border, through the tunnel, in Marc's rented convertible sportscar left little time to talk. For that, she was grateful. She felt a bit awkward with him, still unsure of the scrambled messages her brain kept sending her.

He parked the car, and they walked through several boutiques, eying porcelain figurines and fine bone china. Marc wore mirrored sunglasses and kept his hat pulled low. Puzzled, she asked him why.

"The price of fame. Anonymity is one thing I gave up years ago. It's not as bad as it used to be, but there was a time when teenage girls made my life miserable. I had to hire bodyguards."

She flushed and scrutinized a particular china cup far too long, remembering her own foolish adulation and attempts to get closer to him. "Yes . . . I read about how you had to beat off your admirers with a stick. Tough life."

"Ouch." He winced and flashed her a devilish smile. "I think I've been socked right smack in my vanity. Thanks for the lesson in humility."

She tipped her chin, playfully. "Someone has to defend those poor shrieking girls. Think of the romantic dreams you gave them. It was their duty to adore you."

"Of course, it's not so much that way now. When I switched my music loyalties, lots of things changed for me." Something dark and sad flicked across his mouth, catching Callie by surprise. She sensed a story that he wasn't ready to share. Wisely, she didn't question him. She'd been a cop's wife just long enough to know not to pry; to understand that men held their secrets differently than women.

She began to have fun being with him. He was clever, talkative, pulling her out of her shell little by little, bit by bit, until she felt relaxed and festive, almost dizzy with a silly giddiness she'd not felt in years. *A kid in a candy store* . . . The afternoon shifted from sunlight to dusk, and Callie was amazed when she saw long streaks of shadow fleck over the sidewalks.

"Hungry?" Marc asked. "The restaurant I mentioned is nearby." His hand touched her lightly. She could only nod. Her appetite had grown immensely as she'd settled into the familiarity of his company. The restaurant was French, small and private, their table tucked back in an intimate corner. Once seated, they nibbled on fresh vegetables and crusty bread slices in a relaxed aura of contentment.

"Tell me about yourself." His question caught her slightly off-balance. Their conversation during the day had been bantering, impersonal. Mentally, she backed off.

"Like what?"

"How do you learn to write such beautiful music? And don't be modest."

She blushed and shrugged. "I was born very late in my parents' lives. At times I felt like an intrusion. You know . . . like I interrupted something." She glanced toward him quickly, apologetically. *Now why did I say that?* "Oh, not that they didn't care about me. They really did. But . . .

they were in their sixties when I graduated from high school. I think it was hard for them to relate to me . . . my needs."

She continued, rapidly, before he could respond. "When I was six, Daddy bought me a piano. It was love at first sight." Smile lines softened her mouth. "I took lessons and spent hours composing music. When I got to college, there was never any question about what I'd major in."

Lonely. The word came to Marc while he listened to her talk. Insulated and alone. The walls around Callie O'Ryan were high and guarded. He wanted in. He watched her nibble on a carrot stick, her lips closing daintily over the orange vegetable, and he found himself wondering how those lips would taste. . . . It had been a long time since he'd felt so strongly attracted to a woman.

A waiter placed tureens of hot onion soup before them. She told Marc it was her favorite. It pleased him enormously somehow. He gathered the little pieces of herself she offered, and he saved them, like rare coins. "My mother thought I'd make a wonderful concert pianist," Callie said. "But although I was good, I wasn't *that* good! I'm glad that you like my song, Marc. You sang it so beautifully the other night. I want to hear it again. I was so shocked then that I know I missed a lot."

"I'll give you a private concert whenever you want." His green eyes bore into her, and Callie caught her breath, feeling a pressure inside her lungs. She allowed him to hold her gaze for an extra beat, telling herself, *Back off! This man is fantasy. You're starstruck, Callie-girl!*

The soup course disappeared and something succulent, swimming in sauce and mushrooms took its place. She cut her meat methodically and said, "I'll hate myself forever if I don't ask how you became a musician."

He laughed. "Actually, there was a time when I thought I'd be a concert pianist too. I grew up on Long Island in a house with two pianos and an organ. My mother played for pleasure. I eventually studied at Julliard. . . ."

"I knew it! I knew you didn't just pick up music by ear. There's too much formal technique when you play." She fairly sparkled, gloating over her ability to perceive and judge musical expertise.

His deep laugh mingled with hers. "I thought my father would croak when I put together my band, the Blades. And then when we had the audacity to hit it big on our first try . . . well, I thought he'd have apoplexy."

"Seems odd. I'd thought your family would have been overwhelmed to have such a famous son." The corners of his mouth flinched slightly as she spoke. *That nerve. You've hit that nerve again, Callie,* she warned herself.

"My father's and my relationship is very complicated. It always has been. He chose his words carefully, as if he were picking his way over treacherous ground. "Father grew up believing that people had to pay a price for whatever they earned from life. He paid it, so why not me? It was scandalous to him that I got fame and fortune without ever paying any dues. The life I led, the people I ran with, the money I made—all for just standing on a stage and singing—it sat in his craw like a stone."

"But you became a Christian and everything changed for you. I remember reading about your leaving the band and everything. . . ." She was bewildered, thinking that she'd missed something. As if she'd come in during the middle of a movie and couldn't quite grasp the sequence of events.

Marc lay his fork carefully across his plate, tipped back in his chair and measured her from beneath dark, thick brows.

"You mean you don't know?"

"Know what?"

"Raphael is my stage name. A name I chose when I formed the band. My real name is Rothstein. I'm a Jew, Callie. By heritage, by lineage, I'm a Jew."

chapter 4

SHE STARED AT HIM STUPIDLY FOR A MOMENT. "You're Jewish? I thought I knew everything about you. . . ." The words came before she could check them, causing her to blush furiously.

If he noticed, he ignored it. "It wasn't something I played up over the years. In Christian circles, a 'completed Jew'—a Jew who's accepted Christ—is no news, and in other circles it's ludicrous." He drummed his fingers on the table top. "But to my family . . . it was an unpardonable sin."

His revelation shocked her. "I don't understand." She appraised him through narrowed eyes. "Rothstein . . ." She rolled the name and mused, "There's a department store in downtown Manhattan . . ."

"My father's."

"You're kidding?"

He laughed aloud at her inability to conceal her surprise. "Father and his brother, Sol, founded it after the war."

"It's one of the most exclusive stores in the city. Why, I bought my first prom dress there." She remembered plush carpeting and mannequins draped in silk and mink. "When you started your band, there must have been things written about it. Why don't I recall them?"

"Clever manager. Father wanted it played down. So we did. He thought I'd go belly up in the music world. It rankled that I made more money in the first year than he'd earned in five when building up Rothstein's reputation. I was twenty years old at the time."

Callie sensed an underlying tension in Marc's words, hinting at some rivalry between father and son. "Excuse me for being so thick, but I still don't understand why your being a Christian is so terrible."

"That's because you've never been a Jew." He raked long fingers through his chestnut-colored hair, made richer by flickering candlelight. "Being Jewish isn't like being anything else. It's over three thousand years of heritage and persecution and survival. It's God the Creator handing down stone tablets from Mount Horeb. Laws of life, rituals, habits that have remained unchanged and unaltered by time and tide. It's pride. God chose us to be a people apart from all others."

"When I became a Christian, I felt special and chosen. . . ."

"Me too. But Christ added depth to my Jewishness. He didn't remove it. It was incomprehensible to my father that I could be both."

"And your mother?"

A small muscle worked in his jaw. "She died when I was fifteen. Father's sister, Aunt Sadie, moved in to raise us."

"Us?"

"My sister Rachael and me. She's three years younger, but I was luckier than she—I got out." Again, something flickered in his eyes that Callie couldn't quite read. "I was to have taken over Rothstein's one day. Uncle Sol had three daughters. I was the only son between them."

"And you became a musician, the heartthrob of a million teenage girls. . . ." She teased gently, attempting to lighten his darkening mood.

He did smile, but a wistfulness didn't leave his eyes. "After I confessed my Christianity, Father disowned me."

"You mean he disinherited you?"

Marc shook his head. "Jews don't disinherit exactly. He tore his coat lapels and wailed."

Callie leaned forward, wide-eyed. "Wailed?"

"It's an orthodox custom. It meant that he no longer had a son. Now, it's as if I were never born. My name is never uttered in his house. All traces of my existence have been removed."

Stunned, Callie stared open-mouthed. "You're not serious!"

A sparkle broke through the clouds in his eyes. "I made my peace with it a long time ago. Remember, Jesus said he came not to bring peace, but a sword. To set a 'man against his father' and that 'a man's enemies will be the members of his household.'"

Callie had read these words, but until now, she'd had little cause to dwell on them. Marc continued. "However, I do miss Rachael. She defied father—secretly, of course. She's contacted me. Even came to see me after her son Daniel was born four years ago. Wickedly defiant woman, my sister. She's divorced now—Father's doing."

The family's complex feud was too much for Callie to comprehend. How deep the waters ran beneath the man across from her. She wasn't the only person who had sustained losses. She wanted to reach over the table and touch him. But she didn't. She had no right.

Marc caught her wish to touch him on her face. He saw her check it. He didn't want her pity, but he did want her to touch him. He took the initiative, grasped her hand and squeezed it. "God healed my hurts over my estrangement from my family, Callie. I regret the loss, but I don't mourn it. I have a new life and a new meaning to my life."

". . . unlike you." He hadn't added those words, but she heard them anyway. He'd done it again! Reached inside her innermost mind, into her dark, secret thoughts and exposed them. She winced, and instinctively she recoiled.

Marc lost her. He knew it the moment it happened. She'd locked him out and the walls wouldn't be so easy to scale the next time, he reminded himself. He'd have to be more careful. "You ready to head back?"

"Yes."

They left, not talking during the ride into Detroit. The stars had come out and glistened against the black velvet of the sky. A chilling breeze reminded Callie that spring wasn't yet here. She tugged her coat tighter and hunkered down into the bucket seat of the car. The fairy tale was over and the princess was returning to her former world.

In the hotel parking lot, he helped her into her car, then hunched over leaning his elbows against the open window. "I enjoyed today very much, Callie."

"Me too. Thank you." Silence.

Impulsively, he reached in and lifted her hand. He pressed his lips to the back of her knuckles and a shiver skidded up her spine. It wasn't from the cold. "Shalom, Callie. In Hebrew that means peace. We say it when we tell someone hello or good-by. We part, but we don't part . . . yet always in peace." He stood upright and stepped away.

"Shalom," she repeated tentatively and drove off into the night.

"Callie O'Ryan, you're absolutely radiant! What's happened?" Janette's words greeted Callie as her friend pulled her into the warmth of her house.

"It's merely the March wind hitting my face."

"March wind indeed! Don't you know what happens to little girls' noses who tell fibs?"

"That's little boys' noses." Callie stripped off her coat and headed into the living room where Jill sat at an upright piano, playing the scales.

Janette was not to be put off. "I demand to know how your visit to Marc Raphael went or I swear I'll sit on you and twist your arm until you spill your guts."

Callie threw up her hands and drawled, "Don't hit me Miss Scarlett! I'll tell! I'll tell!"

"That's better." Janette sniffed, mollified.

"He was most gracious to me. He did not threaten me with a counter-lawsuit for defamation of character . . . and he took me to dinner in Windsor."

"You had a date with Marc Raphael?" It was Jill that squealed over that tidbit of information.

"Just a simple dinner to say no hard feelings," Callie cautioned. "Nothing more."

Janette gave her a skeptical look. "So he'll sing your song?"

"Kevin sold it to him. It's what Kevin intended. Now, it's what I want too."

"I can't stand it!" Jill babbled. "Dinner with Marc Raphael! Too much!"

"Get your mind back on your lesson, girl," Callie chided with a furious blush.

"You do look radiant," Janette insisted.

"You're making much ado about nothing."

Melanie poked her head into the doorway. "What's all the shouting about?"

"Aunt Callie had a date with Marc Raphael," Jill began.

"You did?"

"No, no. Stop it! All three of you." Callie stamped her foot emphatically as she faced the enthusiastic bunch of females. "I made peace with him and that's all." *Shalom* . . . The word floated back to her, along with the memory of dancing green eyes. "Now settle down. Jill, back to the piano. We have a lesson. Janette, back to the kitchen. I expect dinner in payment for this inquisition. And Melanie . . ." She gazed down at the child's upturned face. "What did you want, dear?" Her tone softened.

Melanie brightened. "I wrote you a letter. Just like you said I could. Do you think my alphabets are good?"

Callie scanned the proffered sheet of notebook paper, quickly reading the message of childlike patter of carefully shaped block letters. "Very nice, Melanie. Why look how neat your writing is! Thank you."

The blond girl beamed at the praise. "I'll write you some more," she promised, before scooting out of the room.

"She's adorable," Callie told Janette, who stood staring at Callie thoughtfully.

"Merely a simple dinner in Windsor, huh?" The dark-haired woman crossed her arms and added, "Just be careful, Callie O'Ryan, and don't lean over too far. The extra weight of your nose could land you flat on your face."

Callie struggled to put Marc Raphael out of her mind for three days. It wasn't easy. He'd awakened feelings in her she thought long dead. Oh, she'd dated in the years since Kevin's death. But the dates had been diversions at best, disasters at worst. No one had prepared her for those stirrings of pure physical attraction she felt when she was with him. No one had warned her about the care and concern she'd sensed in his voice. "Old crushes die hard," she reminded herself. "It's the legend, not the man." She almost succeeded in shoving him completely aside. Then he called.

"Be my guest tonight at my concert at Cobo Hall."

"Tonight?"

"Afterward, we'll come back to my suite and have a midnight supper. It takes me hours to unwind after a performance. I can't think of anyone I'd rather do it with."

"Well . . . I–I . . . Yes. I'd love too!"

"Good! My limo will pick you up and bring you straight to the hall. Meet me backstage. You can watch from the wings.

Riding in the sleek limousine, Callie empathized with Cinderella. But the car was no former pumpkin. She already knew Prince Charming. And she couldn't conceive of living happily ever after. Still, she looked forward to the evening with spiraling delight. The stage area was a bustle of activity. Marc had only moments before the concert's start to grasp her hands and say, "Sit on that stool between the two curtains. You'll be able to see and hear everything." His eyes burned with blazing intensity, and his body, clad again in black, seemed coiled like a cat's.

Callie did as she was told, letting the music wash over her when he sang. From her angle, she couldn't see the audience, but only Marc and the banks of stagelights that reflected off him and the neck of his guitar. His voice wrapped her in melody, cuddled her, and left her heart uplifted. Later, when he sang "Gifted," she tensed, but suddenly she was able to extricate the song from the past and float with it into the present. *It's only a song. Just a song.*

Marc watched her through the upraised lid of his piano, as she sat perched on the three-legged stool in the wings, her hands clasped in her lap. Clusters of strawberry curls framed her pixy face, made more childlike by a turned-up nose and large glowing brown eyes fringed with sooty lashes. She wore a cream-colored sweater dress of wool and angora. The angora gave the illusion of incredible softness, caressing her slender body like angel hair. It occurred to him that she seemed entranced and it made him want to make her feel that way forever. Enthralled and enchanted. Only for him.

In the years since his conversion, he'd been very careful in his personal life. He had concentrated on his career, thrown himself into rebuilding his reputation as a Christian singer. Together, with Alex, he'd reconstructed his singing career, dedicated his time to learning about Christ, reshaping the man he'd become. It had kept him very busy. Too busy to bother with personal relationships. And for a long time, it had been enough. God had been merciful to him, giving him back his fame and fortune. God continued to bless him, marking his days with grace and abundance.

Marc gave back, generously. It awed him still that he knew Jesus Christ, one on one. Yet, of late, there had been a restlessness, a yearning. He didn't know for what. He only sensed that God had something more for him. Something deeper. It was as elusive as mist. More and more, he thought about the dream, the vision that had begun five years before. Only Alex knew about it and he often urged, "Say the word, Marc, and I'll move heaven and earth to help you accomplish it."

Looking at Callie across the wide expanse of the stage, Marc felt renewed urgings to begin the project, to fulfill the dream. He'd waited, waited patiently for God to give him the sign to proceed. Was the time now? Was Callie the person to make it happen with him? Marc tipped his head, closed his eyes and allowed his voice to whisper the plaintive strains of "Gifted." Her song. Kevin's song. He snapped his eyes open and buried them into hers.

Callie allowed herself to become ensnared in Marc's gaze. It was as if she was being pulled inside him, caught up in a whirlwind. Why was she here? What was happening to her? *Kevin . . . why did you leave me? God . . . where are you?* Emotionally shaken, she pulled herself away. Like taffy, their invisible bond stretched and hung suspended, but unbroken.

"Make yourself comfortable while I take a quick shower. Room service will bring up a cart soon. Just let them in," Marc instructed, striding toward the bedroom of his suite, jerking his sweater over his head as he talked.

Callie followed cautiously behind him over the lush carpet to the sofa. She caught only a glimpse of his broad, muscled back before the bedroom door shut, locking her out, alone in the softly lit suite. The quiet descended over her as she settled onto the cool sofa, her heart hammering. The concert had been perfect. Why had she agreed to come to his hotel room with him? In the cocoon-wrapped luxury of his private domain, the decision seemed foolish, reckless.

Room service arrived with a cart laden with white-linen, silver-covered platters and pale peach candles. She resisted the urge to see what he'd ordered, seating herself at the table for two and peering into the dancing candlelight for what seemed like hours. The quiet began to unnerve her.

Too nervous to sit, she crossed to his piano and played a few notes. Feeling the soothing balm of music, Callie settle at the bench and played in earnest, a concerto, filled with intricate patterns and difficult passages. It kept her from thinking. She closed her eyes and tilted her head, immersing herself in the music.

"Beautiful."

Marc's voice snapped her from her safe haven. He stood over her, his hair still damp from the shower, smelling of fresh soap. Her fingers forgot their purpose.

"Don't stop."

"And let the food get cold?" She asked a little too brightly.

He held her chair, and she waited until he sat across from her. By candlelight, his skin glowed bronze, and the green of his eyes went dark and smoky. He blessed the food and served her. She ate without tasting.

"Thanks for helping me unwind. Performing is a high like no other. It takes a while to come back to earth."

"Eating at midnight makes me feel sinful. When do you sleep?"

"Why waste the time? Consider what happened to Rip Van Winkle."

She felt a desperation to talk about him and not herself, to keep the conversation light and impersonal. "I often wondered how the 'other half' lived. Was it always like this? Midnight soirees and . . ." She picked up the lid from a serving dish. ". . . cheese blintzes."

"No. Before it was hell." His leaned back in his chair, draping his arm over the velvet cushion, his tone gone serious.

Surprised at his frankness, Callie pressed, "But you had all that money and fame. The world adored you."

"Money buys a lot of things, Callie. But not everything it buys is worth having. And people are a fickle lot."

"Well then how did you ever become a Christian?" She asked the question without guile, unable to juxtapose the two kingdoms. She'd come to the Lord so differently. A frown puckered her brow as she struggled to recall the headlines and articles Kevin had shown her. "I remember something about one of your band members. Vince . . . the drummer. Wasn't that his name? Didn't he die tragically?"

Marc rubbed his hand across his forehead. Even after all this time, he found it painful to remember. "We were having one of our typical 'anything goes' parties. The hotel room was crawling with hangers-on, along for the ride. I didn't know two-thirds of them, but I didn't care either. Vince was high on something. He yelled at me from the balcony, 'Hey! Look at me. I'm Superman!' Then he jumped. He thought he could fly. We were thirty stories up."

Callie tasted his anguish, hating herself for making it all come back to him. This time, she allowed herself to touch him, featherlight, along the back of his hand.

He smiled and leaned nearer, letting his finger rest on the pulse of her wrist.

Her walls were down. Her eyes became the windows of her heart, and he saw her vulnerability along with deeply embedded shards of nurtured guilt. Just as he'd had no control over losing Vince, she'd had no control over losing Kevin. But the guilt was there just the same. The insight made him catch his breath. He kept talking, wanting to draw her out all the more.

"After the police and the reporters and the curious left that night, I found myself alone. Totally alone."

Once again her eyes revealed her empathy.

"I found a Bible in a drawer and started to read it, desperate to keep from thinking about what had happened. The first thing I read was Ecclesiastes. 'Vanity of vanities . . . All is vanity.' As a Jew, I'd read it many times. But it was the first time I'd understood it. Callie, my entire existence was vanity."

He held her hand so lightly that she almost didn't feel it. All she knew was that she was linked to him. His faith beckoned to the hollow places in her soul. His voice surrounded her.

"Next, I read the Gospel of Matthew. I didn't know then that Matthew wrote his book especially for us Jews. We aren't forbidden to read the New Testament. But since I'd been born a Jew, I'd never read it before. I met *Yeshua, the Messiah* in those pages. It was electrifying." His voice had dropped to a whisper.

"Jesus, as the rest of the world calls him, was a Jew. Born and raised as a Jew, a salvation for the Jews. I'd seen paintings of Jesus. A lily-white Jesus that belonged to you 'Christians.' But suddenly, I saw a Man who looked like *me*, spoke Hebrew, celebrated the Jewish holidays as did my family. I saw another Jew." Marc pointed back at his chest. "And yet the things he had to say . . . the way he talked about the kingdom of heaven . . . the way he spoke about love." Marc's eyes narrowed with the intensity of his feelings. "I met a Man who was also God. I met the Messiah. And it changed my life forever."

Callie struggled to see Christ through Marc's experience. To touch God vicariously, through Marc's words. She could not. God had cut her off, shunned her, left her in some wasteland over the past four years.

"I wish I could feel that way again. . . ." She said it hesitantly, with detachment.

The haunted look crept back into her eyes, and Marc winced. He watched the shutter close over the window to her heart, helpless to stop it. He told himself to tread lightly. Having opened up once, she might do it again. Mentally, he shifted gears, slid his hand up to her elbow and urged her to stand.

"Come over to the piano. I want your opinion on something." Diversion supplanted introspection.

She followed him, docilely, drained by the intensity of their conversation. Marc sat on the bench and began to play.

"This melody has been running around in my mind for months. Tell me what you think." He bent forward, and she watched his fingers stroke the keys.

She thought it was the most beautiful tune she'd ever heard and told him so. His green eyes danced.

"I'm stuck in one place. Where do you think it should go from here?" He played to a point, crested to a crescendo, and stopped.

Callie frowned, instantly caught up in the musical dilemma, sorting out the possibilities in her mind. She sat next to him and placed her hands over his on the keys, repeating the pattern of notes from memory. The keys felt warm and alive from his touch.

"How about this?" She took the notes to a logical conclusion.

"Very nice! I like it."

His compliment warmed her, rekindling sparks of creativity and revitalizing her after their mind-numbing conversation. *This I can deal with,* she told herself. *This is real.* Her blood coursed as her fingers skimmed over the keyboard, repeating time and again Marc's soaring melody.

His hands joined hers, and he played counterpoint, building and layering the melody with fresh notes and interpretation. When they ended, she clapped gleefully. He hugged her shoulders. She flushed and straightened, suddenly self-conscious over the absolute union the music had brought to them.

"What are you going to do with it?"

He spun on the piano bench, placing his elbows against the keys and looked at her with measured intensity.

"It's the first song in a musical score I've been dreaming about doing for years."

Her interest piqued. "A score?"

"For a play. Callie, I want to put the Book of Acts into a

musical play. Like *Godspell.* And *Joseph and the Amazing Technicolor Dream Coat.* I've thought about it for five years now. People relate to song. Can you envision Paul's conversion put to music?" She could. "I even have the financial backers for the venture."

"Why don't you?"

He shrugged, his shoulders moving easily in a camel-colored sweater. "Time. And lack of initiative."

She scoffed. "No one has more initiative than you."

"That's what Alex, my manager, says." A smile toyed with his lips. "It's a big undertaking. I'd need to shut myself away for months in order to accomplish it—rearrange my concert schedule and personal appearances, totally change my lifestyle while I composed it."

The information struck her hard. She wouldn't see him again. *Ludicrous!* After tonight, she'd never see him again anyway.

"You should do it," she said, hating the thought that she would be cutting herself off from him so completely. "You have a wonderful gift for music, and you should share it."

"There's another reason." He stretched out his lanky frame. His denim jeans hugged his lean hips, and his sweater rode up on his waist, exposing the taut muscles of his stomach. "I don't want to do it alone."

Callie pursed her lips. "I don't understand."

"I need someone to collaborate with. Someone who understands my vision and my music. Someone I have a complete and total rapport with at the piano, who I can bounce ideas off of, who will yell at me if I have a lousy idea, who will challenge me to write the best music of my life."

"Oh, Marc there must be millions who'd give their eye teeth to collaborate with you!"

"I don't want millions." His gaze bore into her with such impact that Callie felt impaled. "I want you."

chapter 5

DUMBSTRUCK, CALLIE SHOT OFF THE PIANO BENCH. Fantasy had gotten all tangled up with reality. The past had joined with the present, and she couldn't separate the two. "You can't be serious!"

He adjusted his position slightly, but restated his offer. "I already know you're a musician, Callie. I'm already singing one of your songs—remember? I know you can do it—we can do it."

"Marc, this is insane." She paced a few steps, her mind still reeling under the tantalizing spell of his suggestion. How many times she had dreamed of hearing those words as a teenager? How many songs had she composed especially for him? God was mocking her! Giving her the desires of her heart when they no longer mattered. No. No! It was impossible.

Marc watched a catalog of emotions cross her face. His own hopes peaked, but fell when he saw her expression settle on rejection. "Isn't it the tiniest bit tempting?" He dipped his head to the side like an appealing little boy.

"I have a job . . . responsibilities."

"Quit. Think of the fame. Your name in lights. The world at your doorstep."

High color rose to her cheeks. "Stop it. I don't want fame."

"All right. Then consider the filthy lucre. This could make you wealthy, Callie." He let his tone grow serious. "I'll be very fair and generous with you. Your lawyer can help mine negotiate the contract."

"I don't have a lawyer."

"You did when you were going to sue the pants off me two weeks ago."

She flushed and stammered, "I–I mean . . ."

He rose and crossed to stand in front of her, placing his hands on her shoulders, flashing her a beguiling smile of understanding. He ran his thumbs along her collarbone. An involuntary shiver shuddered through her. Where his hands rested felt hot, branded. "Don't say no. At least tell me you'll think about it. Pray about it."

Pray about it. A fundamental ground rule for Christians, and it hadn't even crossed her mind! *God and I aren't exactly close anymore, Marc.*

"It could be fun . . . working together."

"I'm flattered, really. But it just seems so farfetched. I mean, writing a musical with Marc Raphael."

"I'm a man, Callie. Flesh and blood. See?" She didn't need reminding. Her pounding pulse bore witness to his masculinity. "I have a dream of a musical play based on the Book of Acts. I want you to be part of that dream. Please pray about it. Let God make your decision."

"Aren't you ever coming back to Nashville?" Alex's voice chided through Marc's phone.

"I'm on a concert tour of the Midwest, remember. It's

just as easy to work out of Detroit than to fly back and forth between Nashville." Marc cradled the receiver against his neck and slipped his gold watch on his wrist, hunching his shoulders against the headboard of the king-sized bed in his suite.

"And about three times as costly," Alex sighed. "Why do I feel like Paul Harvey waiting for the 'rest of the story'?"

Marc chuckled. "Doubters and scoffers. The world's full of them."

"Things worked out with Mrs. O'Ryan, I take it." Alex's tone was matter-of-fact, but Marc heard his friend's underlying question: *How much does Callie have to do with your decision to stay?*

"Half and half."

"I've arranged studio recording time, so which half are you working on?"

"I've asked her to do the musical play with me."

Dead silence. "When you drop a bomb, Marc, old friend, you really drop one. Want to tell me, your trusted agent, what's going on?"

Marc filled him in, facts only. "She hasn't said yes yet, but I'm certainly going to press her on it. She's the right one, Alex. She's exactly what I need to get this thing completed."

"Will you work here in Nashville?"

"That's what I'd plan on."

"Then I'd better clear your spring and summer schedule. How long would you give it?"

"Three or four months to write the score. If we start in April, we can have the play ready to open by next spring."

"A lot of people want to see you do this, Marc. *I* want you to do it. You sure Callie O'Ryan is the right one?"

Marc coiled the phone cord around his finger, watching the play of afternoon sunlight slant through the miniblinds. "I'm sure." He hung up and drummed his fingers absently on the bedspread. Yes . . . she was the right one. He thought again of her vulnerable brown eyes, the curve of her mouth. Music made her come alive, forget her hurts. "Shalom, Callie," he said aloud, acutely aware that he wanted her presence in his life as much for his sake as for hers.

The March day dawned brilliant and uncharacteristically warm. Bright sentries of crocus poked cheerfully through shrinking clumps of old snow, and patches of brown earth spread like a stain across the campus. Callie dismissed her class early, donned jeans and a windbreaker, grabbed her briefcase and headed for the river that wound its peaceful way through the campus.

She spread a blanket on the sloping riverbanks, turning to soak in the generous sunshine, inhaling deeply the bite of the breeze tinged with the promise of spring. Soon, grass would appear, colored chartreuse and citron, and the river would slow to a sluggish crawl once it had gorged itself on the melted snow. The overhead sky sparkled blue and cloudless, and the warm sun beat with benevolence against the crown of her head.

A feeling of wistfulness stole over her. Spring and butterflies and blue skies. They touched some closeted area of her psyche and made her feel her aloneness more poignantly than she had in years. Couples strolled hand in hand along winding paths, lost in each other. Callie dropped her eyes, quickly opening her briefcase and removing a file folder of papers.

She couldn't stop thinking about Marc Raphael and his offer. To write a Christian musical play! It was the opportunity of a lifetime. And yet . . . and yet . . . Her life was ordered now—finally. She had purpose, position, duty, and a measure of fulfillment. Could she shelve all of those things for the excitement and adventure of a few months? And how would she resume all these things again after living out a lifetime fantasy? Would this life be so easy to come back to?

And then there was Marc himself. Callie closed her eyes and rested her head against the tree trunk. His face swam into her memory as effortlessly as taking a breath. She'd already had a dream about him. A passionate dream where she'd lain in his arms and tasted his incredibly sensuous mouth. Where she'd thrust her hands into his thick, silken hair and felt his fingers play over her skin as wondrously as they did the piano keys.

How would it be to work with him day after day? Eat, sleep, talk music with him? How would it be when the task was complete, and he left her life for good? *Leaving*. So far, her whole life had been nothing but a series of leavings. She'd gone to college, and her parents, free of the encumbrances of parenthood, had moved across the country. She married Kevin, and he'd left her with a dark despair that she still wasn't free of. The baby had left her too, in a series of cramping sensations, the smell of anesthesia, the scrape of a surgeon's knife. *"The D & C was a complete success, Mrs. O'Ryan. Your miscarriage was a fluke—shock-induced, no doubt. There's no reason that you can't have other babies."*

"Is this a private party, or can anybody come?"

Callie's eyes shot open, only to gaze directly into the mirror brightness of Marc Raphael's sunglasses. At first, she wasn't sure that she hadn't conjured him up by remembering her dream. The thought made her squirm uncomfortably. She already suspected he was capable of reading her mind. "Have we met, sir?" She attempted to redirect her surprise over his sudden appearance with a quip.

"I seem to recall your face from a recent concert." He flipped his sunglasses to the top of his head and stretched out next to her, lazily propped on one elbow, his other wrist flung over an upraised jean-clad knee. He wore a chocolate brown shirt and a crinkled-linen jacket, the sleeves pushed up to expose his forearms.

"How did you find me?" She was pleased that he'd even come looking for her. Her heart did a staccato dance in spite of her mind's stern inner warnings.

"I called the Music Department. They gave me your class schedule, but your classroom was empty. I immediately diagnosed spring fever for your disappearing act. So I asked some students where the most beautiful place on campus was. They told me, 'the river.'" He wagged a finger at her. "Playing hookey is a no-no."

"We couldn't keep our minds on work when it was such a beautiful day, doctor. 'All work and no daydreaming . . . ,'" she paraphrased. "Say, is this one of the administration's strong-arm tactics to make sure I'm earning my keep? I have ways of keeping my whereabouts secret. What can I do to keep you quiet?"

"That question opens a gamut of choices for me. Do I get three wishes?"

"What three did you have in mind?"

His dark brow arched eloquently. Sunlight streamed through barren branches to gather in glistening pools on his hair and shoulders. "If I tell you what they are, then they won't come true, will they?"

Her pulse fluttered in her throat, and she felt light-headed, as if she'd run too far without stopping for a breath. "Well, if you don't tell, how will I know what they are?"

"Impasse." He watched the subtle play of emotion on her face, knowing that he was affecting her, using her attraction for him to pull her into his life. He was adept at making women bend to his will. In his old life, he'd done it all the time. But he didn't want it to be that way with Callie. He wanted her to want him, need him for deeper reasons. She wasn't a toy designed for his pleasure, but a lovely, vulnerable woman, who clung to old hurts and harbored phantom guilts.

With an abrupt shrug of self-disgust, Marc straightened. "I'm leaving for five days on a tour in the Upper Peninsula. I'll be back at the end of the week." His tone sounded brusque, and Callie wondered why he'd become so suddenly businesslike. "I guess I want to know if you've thought any about my offer. If we're going to do it, I'd like to start by mid-April."

Callie twisted a paper clip into a shapeless tangle and stared purposefully straight ahead. "I've thought of little else. But I still don't have an answer. Marc, I don't even know how to pray about it. Wanting to do it isn't enough. I have to be sure I'm supposed to do it."

"That's true, Callie." Marc resisted the urge to reach over

and turn her chin so that she'd have to look at him again. "Have you thought of asking God for a fleece?"

"A what?"

"Remember Gideon? When God told him that he was the one chosen to deliver Israel from her enemies, he asked for a sign. He left a wool fleece on the ground overnight. If the ground remained dry and the fleece wet, then he'd accept God's summons."

"And the fleece was wet as I recall."

She turned and Marc recaptured her eyes with his and held them. "Of course, Gideon, being a skeptical Jewish boy, asked God to do just the opposite with the fleece the next night."

"The fleece was dry and the ground wet."

A brilliant smile flashed over Marc's face. "If the test was good enough for Gideon . . ." He allowed her to complete the thought. "It must be something unique, Callie. Something special between you and God that no one else knows about. That way, when the answer comes, you'll have no doubts."

Pure skepticism, blended with derision, filled her mind. *God isn't talking to me.* But Marc didn't know that. One look at his face told her that his faith didn't need fleeces. God spoke with Marc Raphael regularly. "I might just do that." She chose her words carefully, so as not to reveal her doubts. "If he answers, I'll let you know."

"When he answers," Marc corrected. "God is faithful, Callie. Of that one thing, I'm sure."

She collected her forgotten papers and shoved them back into her briefcase, gathered her blanket, and prepared to leave, strangely agitated by their discussion.

Marc stood next to her, towering, oddly protective. "I'll call you when I return." He tapped the end of her nose, and she stepped backward. It wouldn't do to allow herself to get too close to him emotionally. It wouldn't do at all.

Marc saw her mask slip back in place and hated it, half wishing that he'd held her, kissed her, forced her to do his will earlier when she'd been susceptible to him. Now the moment was past. Alex was right. Some things he had to leave to heaven.

Rain. It pounded on the window pane in ever-increasing torrents. Callie stood and stared pensively out of her apartment window, watching the deluge wash across the streets and lawn of her apartment complex. "Just like March," she grumbled into the gloom. A clap of thunder caused her to jump. She forced herself to step aside and return to her housecleaning.

A dustrag lay in a forlorn heap on the cherrywood coffee table. She scooted it around without intent. Marc had been gone three days. She missed him. *Stupid!* She had no right to miss him. Yet when he returned, she'd have to tell him something about the play. The melody he'd played for her kept running around in her brain, like a puppy chasing its tail. Words had already come. A verse and then two. *The melody should undergird the entire musical score.*

"Stop it." She pressed her fingers against her temples and wandered back to the window to watch the rain beat morosely against the glass. She traced her forefinger along the cool surface, following a particular rivulet as it streamed to puddle in a gouged indentation in the brick windowsill. She felt like the rain, helplessly flailing against the tide of her life. Maybe Marc was right. Maybe if she asked God for a fleece, he would answer her.

Callie puffed her warm breath onto the glass and wrote the letter *M* in the condensation. "What should I ask for?" *Yellow roses.* The idea floated lazily into her brain, contrasting with the bleakness of March rain. Kevin had always given her yellow roses. They were her favorites, and the only person who knew it was dead. "A fitting fleece, don't you think, Lord?" Because there was no one to give any to her, she doubted they would ever come.

"No matter," she whispered, rubbed the moisture from the window with a swoop of her hand. She would tell Marc she'd asked for a fleece and when there was no answer, he would go away and leave her alone. A tidy way to end it all. She'd be released from his dream. And he'd be satisfied that she'd done all that she could to become involved with it.

"Yellow roses. Lord, if you want me to work with Marc Raphael, then send me a sign of yellow roses."

"Callie O'Ryan! Do you mean to sit there with a straight face and tell me that you didn't jump on that offer like a duck on a June bug?" Janette admonished over her kitchen table.

"I knew I should have kept it a secret. Now you're going to hound me, aren't you?"

"Far be it from me to say another word." Silence fell between them and Callie quietly counted to ten, stirring her coffee, waiting in bemused tolerance. "Well, why not? Why didn't you just tell Marc Raphael you'd write that musical with him?"

Callie laughed, a pure sweet sound that caused Janette to

flush. "Boy when you clam up on a topic, Mrs. Hanson, the silence is deafening."

"Oh, hush! I'm your best friend. Who has a better right to make you come to your senses?"

Callie hadn't told her about the fleece. Stubbornly, she kept it a secret, reluctant to feel foolish in her friend's eyes. How could she confess her doubts about God's presence in her life to Janette? "I still have six weeks of classes to complete. I do have a commitment to the college, you know. And what about Jill's piano lessons? Trying to get her out of practicing?"

"The college can get an interim professor. They'd jump at the chance for the publicity you'd bring them. Why, Farrell could persuade the dean in ten minutes flat to release you for a sabbatical. And as for Jill—she wants to play Little League and would love the opportunity to take a vacation from piano lessons. So what'er your other arguments, smarty?"

Callie sobered. "I honestly don't know if I'm ready to handle something so demanding. I think I'm a little scared."

Callie saw sympathy fill Janette's eyes. "I know you're scared. But what an opportunity! People don't get chances like this everyday." Janette paused, took a breath, and added, "Be honest. It's not the work is it? It's the man."

Their eyes locked. Friend to friend. Woman to woman. A wry smile curled across Callie's mouth. "He makes me feel things I haven't felt in years. He's complex . . . different. I don't know if I want to get involved. And make no mistake—one does get 'involved' with Marc Raphael. With him, it's all or nothing. I know it just as surely as I'm sitting here."

"Could that be so bad? Honey, look at you. You're young and pretty, with a whole lifetime ahead of you. Kevin is gone. He wouldn't have wanted you to mourn forever. The season for mourning is over, Callie."

She stiffened. "I understand what you're saying, but I'm just not ready to jump back in with both feet. Not yet."

The stillness between them was broken when Melanie erupted into the kitchen, followed by a slobbering sheepdog. "Hi, Mom. Aunt Callie!" The child offered a hug, and Callie smoothed her hair.

"Hi, yourself."

"I got a bunch of letters for you. My teacher says I make almost perfect alphabets now."

"Good for you!"

"Melanie, go wash up, and I'll fix you a snack. Your sisters should be right behind you. And take Herman out of the kitchen. The big oaf!"

Melanie skipped out of the room, and Callie helped Janette prepare for the impending onslaught of her daughters, relieved that the conversation between them had ended. She'd said more than she'd intended, revealed more of her feelings. Marc was a problem she wasn't ready to deal with. Yet she was smart enough to realize that no amount of talking about it would make it go away.

The first thing Marc did when he arrived in Detroit from his concert tour was to call Callie and arrange for her to meet him in his suite for dinner. He'd missed her. He hadn't expected that to happen. Yet he found himself thinking of her the entire time he'd been on the road.

"It's just that you're not used to not getting your way,"

he told his reflection in the mirror while he shaved. "She's not falling all over you. She's got you at arm's length, and it's driving you crazy, Marc, old man." He knew there was a measure of truth in the statement. But it was more than that. There was something in her spirit, something in her core that he wanted to touch and hold onto. He'd seen it the first night she'd stormed into his dressing room and threatened him. He'd sensed it every time he tried to get around her carefully constructed walls.

Callie O'Ryan was a puzzle. She wanted, but she didn't want. She got close, but not too close. She gave, but never too much.

Her musical talent was obvious to him. Her inner needs, a total mystery. He wanted her input on the play. They would have an excellent *in tandem* collaboration. But he also wanted that part of her she held in reserve. For what? For whom? Was he the rival of a dead man?

Marc washed off the last of the shaving cream and then splashed cologne across his face. For some reason, God wanted Callie in his life. Confident of that knowledge, Marc jerked a peach-colored polo shirt over his head and raked his fingers through his hair, reorganizing his thick, straight locks.

He turned to leave, stopped, whirled to stare into the mirror, struck by another thought that suddenly shook him. Or was it more that God wanted him in her life? They were not the same thing. Each was different—subtle, but different. One presumed an attitude of taking, the other of giving.

As a Jew, he'd grown up with the idea of *mitzvah*—"divine command." Or, as the prophet Micah had asked,

"What does the Lord require of you?" Marc knew the answer by rote: "To do justice, to love mercy and to walk humbly." Many Jews carried the *mitzvah* to a fine art—performing ritualistic acts daily, doing good deeds, offering human kindnesses and considerations. But wasn't that one of the things Christ had come to change? To make men see that *mitzvah* was an attitude of the heart and not of the mind?

He glowered pensively at the man in the mirror.

A knock on his door meant Callie had arrived. Quickly, Marc let her inside. She looked lovely, casual in slacks and a blouse with billowing sleeves, a cloud of indigo silk. Her fragrance was floral and sweet. He wanted to gather her into his arms, fought the impulse, and settled for a light kiss to her cheek.

Callie felt his lips brush her skin, and she tingled, almost turning her mouth to join with his. She'd missed him. How could that be possible? Yet she had.

"How was your trip?"

"The audiences were terrific. The traveling was the pits."

"You mean a star's life isn't all glamour and autographs?" She fluttered innocent, teasing brown lashes at him.

"If you only knew. Cardboard food. Cardboard rooms. Hours of loneliness. Sometimes I have to check the phone book to see what city I'm in." He took her elbow and guided her over to the sofa, settled next to her and toyed with a comb tucked in her hair. "How have you been?"

"Busy with classes and such."

"I told Alex that 'Gifted' is to be the title of my new album. I also requested that it be released as a single." He gave her the information matter-of-factly because he wanted to know if she still attached the song to her late husband.

Callie shrugged, taken aback. "That's good of you. I'm sure there were other titles you could have chosen. Thank you, Marc."

"It's going to be a hit, Callie. I have a good instinct for the business. How do you feel about its becoming a hit?"

"I once thought no other person alive would hear it. Now, the entire world will. Funny how things work out, isn't it? Kevin would have been so proud. . . ." She cleared her throat and locked her hands around an upraised knee. "But after all, it's only a song."

Marc felt a measure of guilt for trying to manipulate her emotions about the song. She still associated it with Kevin and probably always would. It nibbled at his pride because he wanted her to write songs for him alone.

"How about a little food to take our minds off business?" He rose and changed the subject.

"Sounds inviting. What's on the menu?"

"I ordered duckling with orange sauce and wild rice. And if you're a very good little girl, I'll have them send up chocolate mousse."

"Plying me with goodies? What are you softening me up for?"

His eyes gleamed impishly, and Callie lifted an eyebrow. "Wicked man." Secretly, Callie felt she already knew the answer to her own question. He wanted to know about the musical. But, since she had no direction or response to her prayer, she was determined to put off the topic. Even if he withdrew the offer.

An impatient rap on the door caused a puzzled frown to

cross Marc's face. He glanced at his watch. "Room service isn't due for an hour."

"Probably some lovesick teenager."

"Better not be."

He bounded to the door in long-legged, powerful strides.

Didn't he do anything slowly, Callie wondered.

He jerked open the door, and a small, dark-haired woman squealed his name with a shriek of delight. Callie watched, open-mouthed as she flung herself against Marc's chest and wrapped her arms around his neck with total abandon.

chapter 6

"MARC! DARLING! I've trailed over half the Southeast trying to track you down. When I showed up on your doorstep in Nashville, Alex said you were in Detroit. Don't you ever stay home?"

"Rachael! What are you . . . ? Callie, meet my sister, Rachael Rothstein."

Callie crossed quickly and held out her hand to the dark-haired beauty. *Expensive*. That was the only word she could put to Rachael Rothstein. Her dress was designer, her heels lizard skin, her nails perfectly manicured, long and red. A large oval emerald glittered from her finger. Her hair was dark, like Marc's, pulled back into a severe knot at the nape of her neck, setting off flawless make-up and ivory-colored skin. Her eyes, more hazel than green, were framed by thick mascaraed lashes.

"Come in! How are you?" Marc scooped her against him again, hugging her, as if she might fade away.

"Not so fast, brother," Rachael gasped breathlessly. "There's someone in the hall I want you to meet."

Rachael tugged and from around the side of the doorjam a small child emerged. He was petite, like his mother, not much older than four, with eyes so dark they were almost black and hair that matched. Marc dropped to a crouch and reached out to the boy. "Daniel? Is this Daniel?"

The child clung shyly to his mother's knees. "Now don't be a stranger," Rachael urged. "This is the Uncle Marc I've told you so much about. Remember how we listened to his records together?"

Callie's heart went out to the wide-eyed boy, his lower lip trembling, on the brink of fear and wonder.

"He's talked about nothing else but meeting you, and now look at the way he acts."

"The last time I saw this fellow he was a babe in arms. Where are my manners? Come inside." Marc straightened and led the group to the sofa, where Daniel snuggled close to his mother, absorbing his uncle's aura through fascinated stares. Callie suppressed a smile, identifying completely with the child's awe.

"So you decided to drop in for a visit. Where does father think you are?"

A frown creased the bridge of Rachael's nose. "Disney World."

Marc laughed. "I hope you went so that when he quizzes you, you can make intelligent remarks."

"I have photographs to prove it."

"Did you like Disney World, Daniel?" Callie asked. The boy gave a tentative nod. "What was your favorite ride?"

"The Spinning Tea Cups."

"Are they fun?"

"Yeah. They go real fast round and round. I got dizzy. I went on it this many times." He held up four fingers.

"And I got sick every time," his mother added.

"You're a long way from Disney World . . . and Long Island."

"Not as far as I'd like to be."

"Did you come to see me, or to defy father?"

Rachael rapped Marc across his chest. "This is gratitude for three extra days of travel? Next time I'll write, dear brother."

He hugged her, soothing her ruffled feelings with a nuzzle of his chin to the top of her head. "Don't pout. Shalom. I've missed you."

Marc ordered extra room service. While the four of them ate, Callie listened, fascinated, to the animated chatter between Marc and his sister. Daniel picked at his meal and when his tiny head began to nod, she motioned to Marc.

"Let me put this guy to bed." He scooped the dozing child into his arms.

"He needs his pajamas . . . ," Rachael started.

"He needs some sleep without you hovering over him." They entered the bedroom, emerging in minutes, arm in arm. "Well, of course you're staying here with me. This suite could sleep an army. Where's your luggage?"

"Locked up downstairs in the bell captain's room. I don't want to impose." Rachael's eyes roamed over to Callie, who flushed and squirmed under her look of speculation.

"Callie and I are friends," Marc interjected with an amused twinkle, noting her discomfort. "Actually, I've asked her to collaborate with me on a musical project. I was plying her with charm when you arrived."

"He was plying me with charm when you *rescued* me," Callie corrected.

Rachael glanced back and forth between them. "Timing

never was my strong suit. I'll make it up to both of you somehow."

"How long can you stay? And, seriously, where does father think you are?"

Rachael sighed, kicked off her shoes, and leaned into the sofa cushions. "I told him I needed a vacation. Which is the truth. I said after Disney World I was taking a few weeks to shop and relax in Palm Beach. If it's all right, Marc, I'd like to stay until after the Passover holidays. You know how the holidays are around the house."

Marc rolled his eyes. "I remember. But I don't celebrate Passover any more, Rachael. For me there's only Easter."

Rachael shrugged her shoulders. "You know I've never been a religious Jew, Marc. I don't care what you celebrate. I'd merely like to stay with you the next two weeks. I've missed you."

"My suite is yours." He gestured grandly around the room. "And I've missed you too."

"Won't your father suspect something if you don't come home with a tan?" Callie blurted out her question, caught up in their conspiracy. They resembled a trio of naughty children.

"Good point." Rachael tapped her perfectly shaped nail against her lower lip.

"The sauna!" Callie snapped triumphantly. "This hotel has a sauna and special tanning lamps. I read about it in the brochures."

Marc and Rachael stared at her momentarily, and Callie felt a slow blush creep up her neck. Suddenly, they erupted into simultaneous laughter. "This woman has *moxy,* Marc. Keep her around. I like her."

"I like her too."

Callie grinned sheepishly, aware that her resolve to remain uninvolved with Marc Raphael had been thwarted. Like it or not, she'd become lured into his life once again.

While it took Daniel longer to warm up to Marc, the rapport between Callie and Daniel had been instantaneous. Marc saw it from the first night. Marc spent over an hour helping Daniel play the piano, and when Callie arrived that Saturday, Daniel dragged her to the keyboard with a cry of, "Come see what I can do, Callie!"

The two of them sat on the bench and concentrated on the keys. Marc watched, with a tenderness that startled him. The joyful bubble of Daniel's giggle twisted something inside Marc. He'd known the boy three days and already he adored him. He'd known Callie for only a month. And he wanted her—in every way. Whether they worked together on the musical or not, he would figure out a way to keep her in his life. He hooked his thumb on the back pocket of his jeans to keep from touching her.

"I think your family's going to have another musical genius," Callie announced. She smiled up at a brooding Marc as Daniel beamed, basking her in her praise.

"I can't wait to show Papa."

"Now, Daniel, you know what Mommy told you about keeping our visit to Uncle Marc a secret," Rachael told him from across the room.

Marc's eyes snapped toward her. "Don't teach the boy to lie, Rachael. It's wrong."

"Save the sermon. You know Father would have my head if he knew where I was, Marc."

"Don't let that willful old man dominate your life." There was a harshness in his voice he didn't want.

"Easy for you to say, dear brother. You're out of there! But I still depend on him for food and shelter."

"That's a copout and you know it. My door is open to you any time you say the word."

The air had grown charged between them. Callie slipped a protective arm around Daniel's thin shoulders as Marc and his sister glared hotly at one another.

"If it were only me, it might be different. But I've got Daniel to consider. Rothstein's will be his someday."

"Some legacy!" Marc fired angrily. "In the meantime you live on scraps, handouts from Father's benevolence." Marc almost spat the last word. "Hasn't he controlled and manipulated your life enough?"

Rachael's face went white and pinched. "That's history, Marc. Don't throw it up to me."

Daniel began to whimper, and Callie hugged him more closely, but he'd caught the attention of the others. "You two stop it," she demanded. "You're scaring Daniel."

Marc whirled, saw his nephew's stricken look, and muttered darkly under his breath. Rachael, alarm mixing with anxiety, crossed quickly to hold the boy to herself. "Don't cry, darling. Mommy's sorry. It's not your fault."

"I'm sorry too, Rachael . . . Callie." Marc sounded contrite and deflated, as he dragged his hands through his hair and rotated his shoulders. "I don't mean to take it out on you. But don't let him run your life. You're not a robot, designed for his ownership. And neither is your son."

Rachael gazed up at her brother. "I know. But I can't break away like you did. I just can't." She stretched her hand, palm up. "Please don't let him come between us."

Callie wished she could slip into the crevices of the piano keys. She'd seen and heard things she had no right to hear. Marc offered a terse nod as the muscles in his jaw worked. He turned to Callie. "Forgive us, Callie. Airing the family's dirty linen in front of you isn't very fair."

Fair or not, Callie understood that Father Rothstein was a formidable force, who had shaped the destinies of his clan with an indomitable will. Marc had not broken—nor bent, but had shaken free, and the vibrations were still being felt in the family's life five years later. Thoughtfully, she stroked Daniel's hair.

Over the passing days, Callie found her free time intricately interwoven with that of the Rothsteins'. She became conditioned to the mercurial verbal exchanges between Marc and Rachael. And although their outspokenness sometimes made her breath catch, she perceived that the brother and sister were bound together with the intangible glue of honesty and mutual caring. The first week passed and then the second, until the days of Rachael's vacation had drawn to a close.

"What do you mean the boy's never been to the circus? Is this a child or a miniature adult?"

"Does he look deprived already? He's never dated either. He's only four, dear Marc."

"The circus is appearing at Cobo Hall. I'm taking him. You two women are on your own."

Which is how Callie found herself staring across the room at Rachael with a free day on their hands. "Let's go pamper ourselves! My treat." Rachael announced, twisting her hair into a topknot.

"How do you mean?"

"Downstairs in the salon. Hair, nails, facials . . . the works. Then lunch, saunas, exercise class and a dip in the whirlpool. By that time the men will be home, with Daniel no doubt gorged out on hot dogs and cotton candy." She tapped her toe and grimaced. "If he's sick, I swear I'll make Marc sit up with him all night!"

"It'll cost a fortune to indulge ourselves that way."

"I know," Rachael smiled sweetly. "I'm charging it to Marc."

The hairdresser flounced and fussed over Callie's curls until he'd satisfied himself. She watched her reflection in the mirror, purposely donning a bored expression as if such treatment was a part of her everyday life. Her mud pack dried to a stiff, grey hardness. Callie laughed aloud, cracked the mask, and caused the beautician to shoot her murderous looks.

They emerged from the salon intent on lunch and a sauna. Callie stopped stark still. "Rachael. We went about this backward. We should have done the sauna *before* the hair and facial."

Rachael patted her arm. "Callie, dear, try and think more expansively—more like one of the idle rich. If the sauna messes up our hair and make-up, we'll merely have both done all over again."

"How decadent," Callie gasped in feigned shock.

Rachael's smile was sugary. "Yes . . . isn't it? But what's Marc's money for, if not to spend?"

They ate a lunch of salad and salmon mousse, topping it off with a hot fudge sundae. "How can you do that?" Rachael asked in disbelief as the mound of goo disappeared into Callie's mouth. "I'd weigh a ton if I ate like that."

"It's in my genes," she deadpanned, patting her slacks as Rachael groaned.

They exercised until they ached, baked in the dry heat of the sauna until limp, and slid into the whirlpool with matching moans. "It was all worth it, just for this moment," Callie sighed. The jet stream of water pulsed into the muscles of her lower back as she leaned dreamily against the tiled side of the pool.

"I hate the thought of leaving tomorrow."

"Marc will miss you, and frankly, so will I."

"Will you?" Rachael's plaintive tone caused Callie to ponder the dark-haired woman next to her. She had sounded forlorn, like someone returning to a demanding job after too short a respite.

"Yes, I will. And Daniel too."

"Daniel will miss both of you." Silence and the bubble of the water swirled between them. "So tell me . . ." Rachael's voice took on verve. "Are you going to do that musical play with my brother?"

"I haven't thought much about it lately." It was the truth.

"He'd be a hard man to turn down." Rachael cut her eyes sideways. "Are you lovers?"

Callie sat bolt upright. "Absolutely not!"

"Pity." Rachael sniffed. "If I had a shot at a man like my brother, I'd take it in a minute."

Callie dogpaddled across the small whirlpool, her stomach in a flutter. *Lovers!* Indeed!

"I've seen the way he looks at you . . . your musical ability notwithstanding. And you're not exactly immune to him either. And don't give me that look of innocent denial.

There's something between you two that needs settling." Rachael persisted. "Rest assured—Marc will settle it."

Callie cleared her throat, anxious to squirm out of the harsh limelight of Rachael's intuitive speculation. She'd been curious about Rachael's brief marriage, the innuendo about Mr. Rothstein's involvement in the divorce, and Rachael's retaking of her maiden name. "What about your ex-husband? Is there any chance the two of you will get back together?"

Rachael's expression grew pensive, and Callie felt a small satisfaction that she'd turned the conversation from herself. "He was the gardener. A Princeton graduate searching for himself. I loved him with a vengeance." Rachael smiled ruefully. "The affair began about the same time Marc and Father broke, so Daddy wasn't around to ride herd on me. Richard had been hired to tend mother's gardens. . . ." Her voice took on a wistful tone. "You should have seen my mother's gardens, Callie. They were legendary. Father kept them up over the years as a living monument to her memory. Marc loved them especially. Mother's early death was very hard on him."

Rachael paused, and Callie let the silken water slip through her fingers, watching it splash and bubble in meditative concentration. Rachael threaded her way back to her main story. "We eloped. Father was livid. It took him six months, but he found Richard's Achilles heel. Money. It only cost him ten thousand dollars to persuade Richard to leave me."

Callie gasped. "That's terrible!"

"Was it? Looking back, I realize we would have never made it. The only good thing to come from the marriage was Daniel." Rachael's eyes softened, and she pointed her manicured toe through the roiling surface of the water. "Father loves Daniel. Sometimes it scares me how much he counts on my son. When he's thirteen, his bar mitzvah will be the grandest one in Long Island. That's when a Jewish boy comes of religious age. Father will see to it that Daniel lacks for nothing."

"You—you've never heard from Richard again? He's never seen his own son?"

"Never." Her tone was flat. "We never hired another gardener either."

Callie asked no other questions as Rachael propped her head against the edge of the whirlpool and closed her eyes. Despite the warmth of the water, she felt a chill within. Rachael's loneliness reached around Callie, tentaclelike, and Daniel's cloistered, isolated childhood became a sad reminder of her own.

"Marc! How could you let this happen? Look at the poor boy. What did you let him eat anyway?" Rachael admonished nonstop as she hovered over the whimpering child stretched out on the bed.

Marc's face was a study in concentration and contriteness. "I'm sorry, Rachael . . . I didn't realize he'd shoveled down so much junk."

"See, Callie. Didn't I tell you this would happen? Poor baby . . ."

Callie clasped her hand over her mouth to suppress her amusement. The look on Marc's face and the clucking of his sister were comical. She stepped next to the bed and sat beside the moaning child. "Show me where it hurts, Daniel."

"Right here, Callie." He motioned from his neck to his knees.

"Here's what always made me feel better." She raised his pajama top and rubbed her hand in a smooth circular motion over his swollen stomach. She cooed softly and hummed. In a few minutes, the child had drifted into sleep. "I think he'll be fine," she whispered to Rachael.

"I'll sit with him for a while," she whispered back.

Callie tiptoed out of the room, noticing that Marc had disappeared. Puzzled, she glanced around the softly lit sitting room of the suite when she heard a low groan from the sofa. She crossed to the freestanding sofa in the center of the room, rested her palms across the top of the cushions, and leaned over. Marc lay with his arm shielding his eyes from the golden cast of the 'lamplight, his long, lean body filling the length of the couch.

"What wrong with you?"

"My tummy hurts." He raised his arm and peered up at her from the crook of his elbow. "Will you rub my tummy too?"

"You faker!" She straightened, but he was too quick for her. His hands shot out and captured her wrists. She squealed, but couldn't stop him from hauling her over the top onto his chest. She tumbled against him, her wrists in his viselike grip, her body pressed along the length of his. She stared into his mischievous, glowing green eyes, his face inches from her own, his mouth millimeters from hers.

"What happened to Florence Nightingale?"

"You are incorrigible! Let me go."

"What's it worth to you?"

She struggled, vainly, twisting to break his hold. He

laughed and pulled her even closer. She stopped struggling, took ragged breaths, and stared down into the pools of his eyes. She felt his warm breath against her cheek and caught his spicy fragrance. Something flared behind his eyes, and she felt winded, suddenly conscious of his body beneath hers. He shifted, and she trembled. His long fingers loosened their hold and drifted up to tangle in her hair. Her blood pounded in her ears, and her heart thumped against her ribcage. She recalled his hands on the guitar strings, on the piano keys, and then on her skin in her dreams.

"I–I've got to go." Her voice turned foreign to her own ears.

Marc held her eyes with his, refusing to break his tenuous hold on her desire for him. He saw the tip of her tongue dart nervously to touch her upper lip, felt the involuntary shiver of her body. Her hair was soft . . . so soft. He knew her lips would feel the same. Need flared in him, sharp as a needle, pricking his conscience. "I'm not a school boy stealing kisses, Callie." His voice was husky. "I'll take only what you're willing to give."

For a moment he thought that she might surrender her reserve, lower her mouth and kiss him. But instead, she withdrew, unwrapping herself from his hold and rising to sit beside him. She stared at her hands. "I really should be going."

"Will you come say good-by to Rachael and Daniel tomorrow?"

"I'll phone."

"I'm on the road for the next two weeks." His words were clipped, his eyes hooded. "I can't stay in Detroit much longer. After this tour, I'll have to go back to Nashville."

Callie nodded. He hadn't said: "I'll need a decision about the collaboration." But she heard it all the same. That night Callie tossed, grasping at sleep in fits and snatches. Like an out-of-focus picture, she struggled to sharpen Kevin's image in her mind's eye. But blue eyes kept dissolving into green ones, and Kevin's red beard into the square-cut jaw and cleft chin of Marc Raphael.

Marc didn't call her while he was on the road. Callie wanted him to, hoped that he would, told herself it didn't matter when he didn't contact her. She worked—feverishly, forcing hands and mind to stay busy. She wrote pieces of music, knowing that they belonged in Marc's musical, then shoved the papers into folders in her piano bench with disgust.

She prayed for an answer to dilemma, first asking, "Thy will be done," then passionately adding, "Please say yes, Lord." With everyday that passed her desire to do the musical increased, until it became a gnawing hunger, her longing to work with Marc, a yearning need. Yet, she wouldn't do it without a clear directive from God. As the days passed, her determination to wait it out became obsessive.

One night Callie slept, she became aware by degrees that something was annoying her. A pounding that wouldn't stop, a ringing that wouldn't cease. She startled awake, sitting bolt upright, pushing aside the cobwebs from her brain, knowing that it was her front door demanding her attention.

Once before she had been grabbed from the arms of sleep by a pounding on her door. Her heart thudded as she tugged on her silken robe, and groped for the lamp switch.

"Who is it?"

"It's Captain Forsyth, Mrs. O'Ryan."

"What's wrong? Has something happened to my husband?"

"The bust went sour. . . ."

"Who is it?"

"It's me, Callie. Marc. I have to see you."

Callie's fingers fumbled at the chain, terror propelling her into motion. Her heart skidded to a halt, and she opened the door. He emerged from the night into the light of her apartment, looking drawn, haggard. A day's growth of beard gave his face a haunted aura. "What's wrong? Oh, Marc. what's wrong?"

"My father's dead."

She exhaled her breath, and then slid into his arms, effortlessly. He clung to her, and she rested her head against the smooth nylon of his windbreaker, comforted by the rhythm of his heart. "When? How?"

"He had a stroke. Rachael called . . ." His voice caught.

"Let me fix you some coffee." She pulled away and led him to her kitchen counter where he sat on a tall stool with his fingers thrust through his hair, his elbows propped on the clean white formica, staring into the void. She measured scoops of dark grounds into a paper filter, watching him, hoping for words to comfort him. The water flowed through the coffee grounds, and the aroma filled the room, biting and pungent.

"Tell me about it." She came to him, softly, stopping in front of his stool and touching him along his shoulder.

He turned haunted eyes toward her. "I'd just come off the road. I don't think I've slept for two days. The phone was ringing when I unlocked the door." Her hair was a cluster of curls, around her face, haloing in the light. "I catch a flight to Kennedy Airport in three hours. I've got to go home."

"Of course you do." It struck her suddenly that he'd driven an hour out of his way to tell her personally. The poignancy of his thoughtfulness caused her eyes to mist. "What can I do? The funeral . . . ?"

"It's tomorrow." Her face must have registered surprise because he added, "Jews bury their dead within twenty-four hours, and always very simply. We believe that all men are equal in death. Then we sit *Shiva.*" He reached for her, clasping his hands at the small of her back. She arched against them, absorbed in the sadness of his face.

"*Shiva* is our official period of mourning—a kind of prayer vigil—only for the immediate family. In spite of how he felt about me, I should be there. The customs don't apply to me anymore, you know. But for Rachael and Daniel's sake . . . Aunt Sadie's too . . ." His voice trailed. "Then of course, there will be the rest of the family to contend with."

Callie slipped from his hold and poured them each a mug of black coffee. He took it. She saw steam curl around his face when he sipped. When he spoke again, he looked less tired, more determined. "Uncle Sol and his family will be hovering around like vultures. Someone will have to protect Rachael's interests."

"I don't understand."

"I know, and I can't explain it. Just know that's it's necessary that I go home."

"Can I . . . Is there anything I can do?"

He set down the coffee mug and smoothed her hair with his open palm. "I still want to do the musical. I may need to work on it now more than ever. It makes no difference to me whether we do it in Nashville or Long Island. The family home has a music room—the Blades did all their practicing there in the early days."

She cast her eyes downward to the carpet. "I–I still don't have an answer for you, Marc. I've prayed and prayed, but there's been no answer."

"There will be." His voice was confident, and she looked back at him quickly, feeling his arms tighten around her while a smile played lightly with his lips. His confidence and faith buoyed her.

He ran his hands across her back, the smooth surface of the silk catching on the tip of a callused finger. Steel-stringed guitars left calluses. Slowly, gently he lowered his mouth to hers. His kiss was feather soft. "I have to go." He released her and rose from the stool. "Here's where you can reach me."

She took the New York number and walked him to the door, watching him disappear into the night, as swiftly as he had come. Her heart ached for him, for Rachael, for a dark-eyed four-year-old who'd lost his "Papa." Yearning ripped through her. She wanted to be with them. "Let me go, God," she said aloud. "Why won't you talk to me?"

She gritted her teeth and leaned against the doorjam, acutely aware that sometimes no response was an answer in itself.

"You really should go, Callie." Janette said as the two of them stood in her foyer, waiting for the rain to slack and allow Callie to make a dash for her car.

"I know what I'm doing," Callie replied stubbornly, cinching the belt on her trenchcoat with a tug.

"I hope so. It's been over two weeks since Marc left. He's not going to wait forever, you know."

"I'm going to make a run for it." Callie pulled open the front door, ignoring the truth in Janette's words. "Tell Jill, same time next Wednesday." She darted down the sidewalk, through the splashing curtain of water, jerked open her car door and slid into the bucket seat with a shake of her head. Droplets of rain slung onto the dashboard.

"Keys. Keys. Where are my keys?" She muttered and fumbled in her coat pocket, biting back the hard lump of frustration that had settled in her throat. *Two weeks and no answer. Why, Lord? Marc, . . . I miss you.*

Her hand closed on the cold metal keys and a crumpled sheet of paper. *Melanie's letter.* "It's my last one, Aunt Callie. My teacher says I write perfect now. The best in the class." The child's proud words echoed back to Callie. Ashamed that she hadn't bothered to look at it in the house, Callie carefully unfolded the crumpled notebook paper. Simultaneously, she inserted the ignition key and flipped on the wipers and the defroster.

She got no further. Callie gaped at the paper in stunned silence, her breath trapped in her lungs, unable to escape. She heard the monotonous swish of the wiper blades, the hiss of the auto's fan, the droning of the rain against the metal roof.

The letters on the paper were big, block ones, neatly

formed and perfectly shaped. The message was ordinary—no different from others Melanie had written. The paper smelled of pencil lead and this time, wax. For at the bottom of the page Melanie had drawn a picture—a flower. To be exact, a rose. It gleamed off the paper in a riotous splash of crayon . . . round and plump. And yellow.

chapter 7

MARC WATCHED CALLIE WALK THROUGH the airline terminal's long tunnel while deplaning passengers flowed around her, never losing sight of her despite the surging crowds. She was here. Actually here, in New York. Until now, he hadn't believed she'd show—even when she had called the week before and said, "I'm coming."

He felt the tension between his shoulders ease and the knots inside his stomach untie. *She's lovely.* Had it only been a month since he'd seen her? It felt more like a lifetime. What was it about her that touched him? He'd known more beautiful women, embraced more willing ones. But there was something about Callie O'Ryan that rubbed against his soul and caused need and tenderness to flare and war within him.

He smiled as she approached. She reminded him of a kid opening a roomful of presents on her birthday. Her brown eyes danced and sparkled, and her strawberry curls clustered in loose abundance around her face. Her white suit, crisp and linen, was accented by a jewel-bright crimson blouse with a soft bow at the hollow of her throat. He wanted to take her into his arms and kiss her. Instead, he lifted his mirrored sunglasses and said, "Welcome back to the Big Apple."

Callie could scarcely control the pounding of her heart as she drew nearer to Marc. Everything was happening too fast. Ever since she'd called him and said, "I'm coming," her life had taken on a carnival atmosphere. There'd been so many loose ends to tie up, so many things to organize in order for her to come spend the next few months in his family home as guest and co-worker. *Thank heaven for the Hansons!* Without their help, she could not have arranged things so quickly.

Callie felt flutterings of anticipation in her stomach. Marc wore cream-colored linen trousers and a matching loose-fitting jacket with the ever-present sunglasses and a fedora pulled low over his forehead. She recalled the feel of his mouth on hers in the brief kiss they'd shared in her living room and blushed. "It's good to be here."

He brushed his lips across her forehead and gave her shoulders a brotherly squeeze. "Let's get moving before we're trampled. Give me your claim ticket, and I'll send the chauffeur for your luggage." He took her arm and led her confidently through the tide of humanity, out into the bright April morning sunlight to a waiting sleek gray limousine.

She sucked in her breath as she settled into the lush velour upholstery, instantaneously enveloped in the cool, quiet air of the car's interior.

"How was your trip?" Marc turned to face her, discarding his hat and thrusting his fingers through his hair.

Her fingers wanted to do the same. "Wonderful. But I still feel like I'm flying. Is this thing for real?" She ran her palm across the car's plush cushions.

"It's one of the family cars. Ostentatious, huh?"

"How many are there?"

"Six. You can pick out the one you want for your personal use."

"You'll corrupt me." She fingered the polished burlwood paneling and tapped the chrome handles of hidden compartments.

Marc smiled devilishly and tugged on a lock of her hair. "You're reading my mind, Ms. O'Ryan. It's my intent to corrupt you."

She'd missed him. "How are you, Marc?"

Her question had a deeper meaning, and he knew it. He inhaled deeply as he answered. "It's been a rough month. My father's buried and life's gone on, but it's been very hard on Rachael and Daniel. Harder on Rachael than I ever imagined. He never let her grow up, you know. Kept her as 'his little girl.' I don't know how long it'll take for her to heal."

A lump rose to Callie's throat at the empathy she felt with Marc's sister. "Healing can take a long time . . ." She stared out the window, seeing nothing through the smoked gray glass.

Marc swore at himself for letting the old demons nip at her and deftly changed the subject. "So what did you do with your worldly possessions? Or did you ship them separately?"

"I sublet the apartment, including all my furnishings. If they're demolished, I'll buy new things. After all, you're paying me enough." She cocked her head and let gratitude soften her features. "The contracts were more than generous, Marc. I only hope I don't disappoint you."

"You may be less enthusiastic when you find out what a taskmaster I am to work with."

"I don't believe a word of it."

"I'm a descendent of Moses, you know. He had a reputation for herding people."

She moaned and wrinkled her nose. "I'll let that one pass."

The chauffeur slid the glass partition open between the car's two compartments. "Where to, sir?"

Marc turned to Callie, "How'd you like to celebrate with a side trip to Rothstein's. We'll have lunch with my Uncle Sol in the executive suite."

"Are you serious? I'd love it!"

With the decision made, Callie gazed out the window, watching the New York skyline loom larger as they neared Manhattan. It had been years since she'd left this city. Yet its special magic still touched her. She pushed aside the dark and hurting memories of her time with Kevin and locked onto the ones from her youth. High school, Rose Ann, Madison Square Garden, and a concert by the wild musical sensation, Marc Raphael. She slid him a sidelong glance. Could this really be happening to her? Could she really be riding down the streets in a luxurious limousine next to the idol of her teens?

"Why are you smiling?" Marc had caught her expression. It was as if she knew a secret, and he didn't.

"I feel wonderful!" Callie countered. "I can't believe this is happening to me."

"Oh, it's happening all right." His grin was crooked. "Someday you'll have to tell me about the fleece you asked God for," he said. She'd mentioned it on the phone. "It must have been some message."

"Maybe someday I will." She was purposefully vague. God's communication to her was still too wondrous to share—even with Marc. God meant for her to be here, meant for her to be in Marc's life. Impulsively, she kissed his cheek.

He smoothed her cheek with the back of his hand. It took all of his control to keep from pulling her against himself and burying his mouth in hers.

The car slid to a halt, and the chauffeur opened their door with a flourish. Callie almost gawked at the prestigious stone and black marble façade of Rothstein's. Marc led her through the brass-trimmed revolving door and into the fantasyland of one of New York's finest department stores. It was as she remembered it.

A mammoth chandelier, ablaze with lights, refracted and magnified by the crystal facets, hung suspended from the store's vaulted ceiling. Dove gray carpeting, bordered with a burgundy leaf pattern stretched across the spacious aisles, past clear-glass, gold-trimmed display cases through free-standing brass racks of unique and exclusive clothing. The merchandise was clustered, spread out in a fan design that beckoned the shopper from one intimate setting to another.

"You gave all this up to sing songs?"

Marc laughed. "Retailing holds no allure for me, Callie. I know the business inside and out, but it isn't what I wanted to do with my life."

"Who'll get it all?"

"Daniel, I hope. My grandfather got his family and most of his fortune out of Germany in the late thirties. The political air didn't suit him. He financed this store for my father and his brother Sol. They've shaped both its policies and style ever since Grandfather died." Marc shrugged, and something akin to determination settled into his eyes. "It was Father's wish that Daniel inherit it. Sol and Aunt Barrie are balking at the prospect."

"But Daniel is only a child . . . ," Callie observed.

"And Uncle Sol's favorite son-in-law has his eye on the presidency."

Callie suddenly understood another reason why Marc wanted to remain in New York to work. He was looking out for Daniel's interests. How much must be on his mind, she thought. All the family problems, the death of his estranged father, a musical play to be written in three months . . . She looked at him with renewed respect and growing tenderness.

"Come on." Marc took her hand and pulled her to ornately carved, ivory-painted double wooden doors where the words "Fur Salon" were etched in brass scrollwork. "Let me show you where Rachael and I played when we were kids."

The exclusive salon was a world in itself. The carpeting was pure white. A sitting area, complete with two red Chinese loveseats, a porcelain inlaid ginger jar lamp and a hand-knotted Oriental rug, promised comfort and seclusion. A black lacquered coffee table held an array of magazines, a porcelain tea and coffee service, and a platter of fresh fruit and confectionaries. One wall was solid mirrors while another held three doors that Callie realized would open into dressing rooms.

A tall, graceful woman in her fifties emerged to greet them. Her hair was white and piled atop her head, her dress, blue silk, her manner genteel, cultured. If she recognized Marc, she didn't show it, offering only a gracious smile. "Welcome to Rothstein's, sir. Perhaps I may help you. I'm Mrs. Siegel."

Marc scanned the elegant surroundings with casual nonchalance. Callie tried to keep her eyes from darting everywhere at once. What on earth did he have in mind?

"I thought I'd like to see something in furs for the lady here." His accent had turned decidedly Texan, and Callie shot him a warning glance.

"Of course, sir. Would you like it shown by one of our professional models? Or would the lady care to model them herself?"

"Oh, I don't think . . ." Callie got no further.

"Why don't you send out a couple of honeys to show us your goods, and then the little lady here can pick what she'd like to try." Marc took Callie's hand and pulled her next to him onto the sofa to stop her protests.

"Is there a particular kind of fur you'd be interested in?" Callie admired Mrs. Siegel's composure. She never flinched under Marc's brash Texan imitation.

Impulsively, Callie decided to play along. "Well, I'm very tired of mink. It's so common now. Don't you agree?" She flapped her lashes at Marc, and he nodded in bland consent.

"Rothstein's prides itself on the unusual," Mrs. Siegel said.

"Red sable and chinchilla will be okay." Marc dismissed her with a wave of his hand.

Callie rolled her eyes, and as soon as Mrs. Siegel stepped into another room, she whirled to face Marc. "You're outrageous! What if she finds out we're playing a game with her?"

"My father used this technique all the time. He'd come into a department and act like a customer. If he got perfect service, the employee was rewarded. If not, she was fired. 'Rothstein's sells service, not just merchandise' . . . so consider this a test."

"You and Rachael used to play here?" Callie craned her neck, trying to imagine two children in the intimidating salon.

"In the back, between all the fur coats. We pretended to be Indian warriors hunting game and making clothing from the skins of wild beasts." His little-boy expression made Callie giggle.

Mrs. Siegel emerged with two models, tall and willowy, swatched in red-toned fur from neck to knees. Callie heard her breath escape as her eyes rested on one coat of thick, rich fur.

"The lady will try that one," Marc said, never taking his eyes off her. Mrs. Siegel held the magnificent coat open and Callie slid into it, hugging the silken lining close. She turned to the mirrored wall and gazed, dumbstruck at her image. The fur brought out the reddish highlights of her hair, and her brown eyes sparkled under the magic of the wrap's enchantment. "How gorgeous!" she whispered, running her hands up the downy soft sleeves.

Marc imagined snowflakes on her hair and eyelashes and on the tips of the fur. He stood, faced her and spun her slowly, stopping her when she'd turned full circle. He pulled up the collar of the coat, until it rubbed her cheeks. She slid her hands up to touch his, resting under the collar.

Their eyes fused and Callie felt herself tremble on the brink of some shining abyss.

Marc wished to hold on to that moment forever . . . that moment when he saw her need for him in the velvet depths of her eyes. It was a need that transcended the physical, reflecting the hunger in her soul, and he would have traded his fortune if they could be alone right then.

Mrs. Siegel discreetly cleared her throat. "The lady likes the coat?"

Callie stepped backward, away from the dangerous emotional precipice that had her teetering on its edge. *I can't let myself feel this way. In three months it will all be over.* She couldn't lose again. Not again.

Marc saw her walls go up and became irritated with Mrs. Siegel. "It's all right," he snapped, then glanced at his watch. "I have an appointment. Perhaps some other day." His accent was gone, but no one noticed.

Callie slipped out of the coat and into her too bright smile, desperately trying to control the erratic beating of her heart. *Too close. Too close.*

Marc ushered her out into the main store and toward the elevators. "Uncle Sol eats precisely at noon. We shouldn't be late." He felt ashamed that he'd acted angry. The fur escapade had begun as a game, a bit of fun. It wasn't Callie's fault that he wanted more from her emotionally than she could deliver. She was here, in his life. He would be satisfied with that much. At least, for the time being.

"Hello, Marc." The man who greeted them in the lavishly furnished executive suite was tall and thin. His features were sharp, hawklike, his clothing immaculate, perfectly cut. He was almost bald, but his eyes were so dark and riveting that Callie didn't notice anything above his eyebrows at first.

"Uncle Sol." Marc nodded, offering a brief handshake. The two men regarded one another warily, as two predators surveying a mutually coveted piece of turf. "May I introduce Callie O'Ryan. She's just flown in to start work with me on a new musical play."

Uncle Sol stiffened. "Then you'll be staying on at the house?"

"Yes. At least through the summer. Maybe longer."

Sol Rothstein measured Callie briefly and murmured a greeting that never made it to his eyes. He gestured toward a marble-topped table near a set of curtained windows. For the first time, Callie noticed the aroma of food from silver serving platters on the table. "Lunch is ready."

The three of them sat in uncomfortable silence while they passed the platters and placed food on Lennox china. "The food's kosher," Sol commented dryly.

"I don't adhere to the old dietary laws, Sol, so it doesn't matter to me."

The air had grown charged between them. Callie squirmed, hearing the underlaying bitterness in Sol's comment. "Should Barrie and I come out to the house for a visit . . . ?"

"The kitchen's kosher, Sol. Rachael and Daniel still live there, and Mrs. Kaufman is still in charge of the household." There was a pause before Marc asked, "Is Sadie enjoying her cruise?" He explained to Callie, "Sol sent his sister on an extended vacation. She needed the rest."

"I'm sorry I won't get to meet her." Callie nibbled on the baked chicken breast without much appetite.

Sol said, "She wired Barrie from Nassau. She's having a good time." The small talk dissipated between them.

"Since you'll be at the house all summer, I assume I won't have to go out there every week to check on things."

"I'll look out for my sister—and Daniel." His tone held an implication evident to each of them.

Sol's smile was tight. "I wouldn't want it to be too much of a burden on you . . . what with your music and all."

"No problem." They finished the meal quickly, and Sol walked them briskly to the door of his office, excusing himself for an afternoon meeting. Alone in the elevator, Marc spoke, breaking the awkward silence. "As you can tell, I've not exactly been received with open arms into the family fold."

"Will it change?"

"I doubt it. The gulf between us is very wide." Marc released a deep sigh. "Try to imagine where Uncle Sol's coming from, Callie. For two thousand years Christians have hated Jews. They've persecuted us as a nationality from the Roman Empire to Nazi Germany. It's Israel against the *goyim*—the Gentiles. For the Jews, the name *Jesus* meant annihilation."

"But that's not true Christianity."

"You and I know that." Marc's hand absently brushed aside her hair. "But the Rothstein frame of reference is Zionistic. They've never met Jesus, but he's the enemy. Therefore, to them, I'm a traitor . . . to my heritage and to the family name." His hand rested lightly against her shoulder. "Yet I know what God has required of me. And I can't go back on his requirements. Not for anyone."

She nodded, understanding instantly what he was telling

her. Kevin had kept his commitments even when his heart wasn't in them. He paid for it with his life. Callie shrugged off the past, thinking back to the luncheon, the tensions, the undercurrents, the subtle power play between Marc and his uncle, acutely aware that she'd been on the battlefield of an undeclared war between men who were not quite enemies.

The Rothstein estate on Long Island looked like something out of the movies. Callie peered, awestruck from the car window at the stone house, swatched in newly greening ivy, as the limousine wound its way through massive iron gates, up a shale driveway over the vast bright green carpet of Winter Rye grass. The house stretched impressively across the lawn, three stories of cobblestone, gables, and a Victorian roofline. Curtained windows, shut against the sunlight, made it look brooding and lonesome.

The car pulled to a halt in front of a veranda supported by massive stone columns, surrounding a doorway that dwarfed even a tall man like Marc. "Not bad," Callie sniffed with faked nonchalance. "No trumpets to announce our arrival?"

"Too strict a union. Besides, they don't play for bar mitzvahs or homecomings."

On the veranda, Marc fumbled with the brass door handle, and Callie let her gaze wander up to the solid brass doorknocker, embodied as a German lion. To the right of the door, fastened to the post, she saw a small metal case, about three inches in length. "What's that?"

"A *mezuzah*. The Bible commands Jews to keep the Law of the Lord upon our doors. There's a tiny parchment inside with the first fifteen verses of Deuteronomy on it. To the Jew, it's a constant reminder of God's presence."

Callie wondered privately how he kept the Jewish and Christian parts of himself separated, sensing again how profoundly his break with Judaism must have affected his family. The front door swung open, and he ushered her into the foyer of his family home. An Oriental rug sprinkled with garlands of pale blue flowers encircling amber-colored medallions graced the polished oak floor.

Callie's eyes adjusted to the dimness. *Marc's home* . . . The idea moved her as much as the house's grandeur. What had it been like to grow up in a place like this? She remembered her own childhood, lonely, insulated, her parents too busy, too centered on their own needs, to consider those of their little girl. She remembered her home with Kevin—an apartment really—but still a home, furnished with orange crates and early Goodwill Industries. The apartment back in Michigan . . . strangers lived there now, and she had no home. All at once Callie felt suspended in time, caught between two worlds, living in neither one place nor the other.

Marc watched Callie survey his family house, sensing the edge of melancholia in her scrutiny. Did she miss the safety of Michigan? He grew acutely aware that she was a stranger here. Everything was different, new for her; he was the only familiar thing, the only constant. By bringing her to him, he'd cut her off from all she knew, clung too, protected herself with. For the briefest moment, her guard was down. She looked vulnerable and afraid.

"Marc! Callie!" Rachael erupted from a doorway and threw herself into Callie's arms. They hugged, and when

Rachael backed away, Callie almost gasped audibly. She wanted to say, "You look wonderful!" but didn't trust her lips to mouth the lie. In reality, Rachael looked thin, drawn, almost frail. Large dark circles, partially concealed by make-up, hovered beneath her eyes. "I can't believe you're here! Oh, I'm so glad to see you."

Callie believed her, for her hold was viselike. "Where's my favorite four-year-old?"

"Daniel's upstairs. His bedroom adjoins mine, and I had the room next to ours fixed up for you. Marc, bring Callie's bags."

Marc shrugged goodnaturedly at his sister's clipped command, scooping up the suitcases and following Rachael up the carpeted staircase to the second floor. Callie bounded up behind them, grateful that Rachael seemed so glad to see her. Their noisy arrival in the hallway brought Daniel out of his room on the run. He all but collided with Callie, stopping, suddenly shy at his display of emotion.

Callie reached down and tousled his dark hair. "Hi, fellow. How are you?"

His dark eyes turned upward, and she felt her heart melt. "I can play 'Twinkle, Twinkle, Little Star' with both hands and sing at the same time," he said.

Callie laughed. "That's better than I can do." Daniel beamed, scrapping the toe of his sneaker across the pale rose-colored carpet.

Marc watched them, seeing Callie's innate love for children brim in her eyes. She would make a wonderful mother. . . .

"Now let Callie get settled into her room," Rachael told her son. "Mrs. Kaufman serves supper promptly at seven.

And woe be to him—or her—who is late." She rolled her eyes in mock fear.

"That's the truth," Marc confirmed. "Why don't you get acquainted with your room, Callie? Change, get comfortable, and then come downstairs and I'll show you around this old barn. I especially want you to see the music room, since that's where we'll be spending most of our waking hours."

Marc deposited her luggage in a room, ushered Rachael and Daniel out, and shut the door behind him. Callie wandered the spacious room that would be her home for the coming months, touching the Chippendale furniture pieces, half-expecting them to dematerialize if she blinked. Petite roses climbed on a pale ivory-colored background of wall paper. An enormous four-poster bed, draped in old-fashioned chenille, stood so high off the floor that Callie's feet didn't reach the carpeting when she perched on the edge of it. An adjoining bath, with a freestanding white porcelain basin and matching claw-footed bathtub, made her feel she'd slipped back in time, to days when chambermaids drew bath water for pampered heiresses.

Quickly Callie unpacked, hanging her clothing in cedar-lined closets and filling the turn-of-the-century wardrobe with her sweaters, lingerie, and personal items. In an hour, her room was neat and ordered . . . and lonely. She quickly ran a brush through her tangle of strawberry-colored curls, freshened her make-up and went to look for Marc.

After peeking into several quiet rooms filled with overstuffed furniture and heavy, closed drapes, she found him in the house's library. He squeezed her hand, flashed her an appreciative look, and led her into a basement area to a door that opened into a sound lock and through another door that revealed the music room.

"Some layout," she said, taking in the two pianos, a cluster of guitars, a keyboard, a set of drums, and a sitting area with efficiency-style kitchen.

"The Blades and I got our start in this very room." Watching his eyes fill with memories, Callie recaptured her original fantasies of Marc Raphael.

Marc crossed to a piano and played the melody line of one of his most famous rock songs. Callie sat beside him on the piano bench and hummed, transported to a distant past. He changed the tune abruptly, picking out the notes of "Gifted." Callie felt the words stick in her throat. *Kevin's song* . . . Yet hadn't it brought her and Marc together?

Marc continued to play, aware that he was hurting her, but it was a hurdle he wanted her over. She had to write for him now. Ghosts and haunting images couldn't intrude in their working relationship. He needed her free of the past if they were going to be a viable team. "Are you all right, Callie?"

She dropped her gaze. Pulling out of her reverie, she was hit suddenly by the enormity of what she was undertaking. "I–I think I'm a little scared," she confessed.

"Of what?"

"Oh, Marc! Are you sure I'm the one to do this with you? I–I just don't know if I'm good enough. . . ."

He stopped playing and took her by her shoulders. "Callie, this musical is very important to me. It's the culmination of all my years as a musician. It's my witness as a Christian. I want to write music that counts, that glorifies and honors God. I know there's a lot going on around here right now. But I know that I'm supposed to do this—just as certainly as I know you're supposed to do it with me. Please believe that."

The green fire of his eyes made her catch her breath. He was so intent on his purpose, she felt the heat. She managed a weak smile. "If you say so, boss."

He didn't return her smile, but lowered his hands to the keys again and played an impromptu line in a minor key. "Callie, you've got to trust me. I won't hurt you. I only want what's good for you."

She felt an infusion of adrenalin, a rush of blood to her head. *Trust.* What did he mean by that? Through the past four years, she'd jealously guarded her feelings, her longings, kept her pain wrapped and buried in a shroud of activity and busyness. "Of course, I trust you. . . ." She said the words mechanically.

Marc looked as if he wanted to say, "No, you don't." Instead he gave her hands a brotherly squeeze and told her, "It's time for supper. Rachael wasn't joking when she said Mrs. Kaufman doesn't tolerate tardiness at her meals. She's the perfect Jewish mother and absolutely kosher." He kept up a stream of patter while leading her back into the main part of the house. By the time they reached the dining room, Callie's anxiety had evaporated, drifting away in the soothing wash of Marc's honeyed voice and mellow laugh.

chapter 8

BY THE TIME DINNER WAS FINISHED, with everyone still seated at the large, oak dining table, spread with delicate lace and set with fine china and heavy elaborate silver, Callie had an excellent idea of what it meant to eat *kosher*. Certain meats were forbidden as food, animals had to be killed according to a specific ritual, and meat and milk were never served together. Even Daniel drank water with his serving of roast beef.

Mrs. Kaufman was indeed a formidable force, heavyset, with a bosom of comfortable proportions and a personal mission that no one seated at the table should weigh less than herself. "You eat this, Rachael," she clucked over every morsel on Rachael's plate. And to Daniel, "Is that all? Why, birds couldn't exist on such fare!" Even Callie didn't escape her ministrations. "You call that a portion? Where did you get this child, Marc? Don't Gentiles eat?" Only Marc was spared her constant dose of well-intentioned mothering.

The family tolerated her hovering, eating only what they wanted despite her urgings. Still, Callie found the food delicious—if a bit overdone—and several times wanted to tell Rachael to eat more too. She ate hardly anything, making an elaborate display of pushing the food around on her plate, but consuming very little of it.

"Will you play some music with me, Callie?" Daniel asked eagerly over his slice of apple pie.

"Hush, son." Rachael chastised. "Callie's here to work, not entertain you."

"Oh, but I'd love too," Callie quickly countered. "After all, we won't start tonight, and I'd love to spend some time with Daniel." It was the truth. What was it about the child that so tugged at her heart strings? His round, dark eyes sparkled as he scrambled from the table.

"I have a piano in my room," Daniel said. "I'll go wait for you.

"Don't be such a nuisance! Can't you see she's hardly finished with her meal?" Awkward silence fell as tears threatened in Daniel's eyes. Rachael sighed. "Mommy's sorry, son. Yes, go to your room. I'll tuck you in later."

The boy retreated, and Callie murmured a quick good-by to follow him. His room was decorated like an Indian fort, and Callie was stunned by the amount of things this four-year old child possessed. A television, two full-sized video-game machines, a spinet piano, and toys of every size, shape, and description all but crowded out the bed in one corner. The closets, large enough for a dresser, boasted shelves crammed with books and games surrounding a generous play area on the floor. A spate of old memories came to her. When she was a child, her room had been much the same way: filled with everything money could buy, but devoid of people.

"Listen to this," Daniel said as he climbed onto his piano

bench where he played and sang his memorized tune. Callie spent the early part of the evening with the boy, encouraging his music, playing board games, and finally, reading him a story. Rachael poked her head in the doorway at eight o'clock, demanding toothbrushing and bedtime. Daniel protested but obeyed.

Once he'd left, Callie turned to his mother. "He has plenty of toys."

"His grandfather spoiled him rotten." Rachael stooped to pick up a heap of discarded clothes and sneakers. "What does a child need with so much stuff?"

"He . . . doesn't talk about his friends. . . ."

"He's only four, Callie." Rachael shrugged in dismissal.

"But doesn't he play with any other children? How about a nursery school program a few days a week?"

"Father always said there'd be a lifetime of school. He'll start Hebrew School when he's six. What does he need a bunch of friends for? Look around . . . he's got plenty to keep him entertained."

Callie suppressed her vexation over Rachael's inability to see how cut off and isolated she was keeping her son. "But a child needs friends. . . ."

"Callie, dear, I know you mean well. You're a sweet friend. But you've never been a mother. You couldn't possibly know what a child needs." Rachael smiled indulgently and patted Callie's shoulder.

Callie felt as if she'd been kicked in the stomach. No, she'd never been a mother. But almost . . . *"Your miscarriage was a fluke, Mrs. O'Ryan. . . ."*

Daniel came into the room and tugged on her hand; Callie bent to kiss his cheek. "Good night, sport," Impetuously, the boy hugged her. She went to her room, the clinging feel of his tiny arms fresh in her mind. She dressed for bed, suddenly tired and drained, not wanting to see anybody again that evening, content to slide between the cool sheets, the memory of Daniel's laughter ringing in her ears. She had made him happy—however briefly, she had made him happy. She fell asleep wondering how many times he'd been happy in his brief, four years in this house.

The fresh, clean scent of early morning and the dappled pattern of sun on cobblestone brought Callie outside into an overgrown garden area the next day. She glanced around perimeters that had obviously once enclosed an intimate, formal garden.

"Good morning, Sunshine." Marc greeted her from a cement bench, inlaid with tile. His eyes glittered like green jewels, and overhead oaks sprinkled leaf shadows over his dark hair. Her heart lurched and she smiled, feeling the comfortable calming his presence always brought to her spirit.

"Good morning yourself." She sat next to him on the bench, inhaling the subtle spice of his aftershave mingling with the sun-bathed air. "I thought I was the only one awake."

"I've always been an early riser when I'm not on the road and giving late concerts. Mrs. Kaufman is slamming around the kitchen, but I managed to escape with a carafe of coffee. Want some?"

Callie poured a cup from an insulated jug and sipped the rich, black brew. "Delicious." She glanced around the tangled, weed-infested flower beds. "Where are we?"

"This is what's left of my mother's once-famous gardens."

"Rachael told me about them. They must have been very beautiful."

"They were. She kept them herself, working for hours each day in the spring and summer. She never allowed any of the gardeners to touch them. When I was a kid, I used to come and visit with her while she pruned and dug and planted. We'd talk." Marc leaned back on his hands, staring up at the blue sky. The muscles rippled in his forearms. "After she died, I still came out here. Somehow, I always felt closer to her here. Since I've come back, I come out here to pray and talk with God. It brings him closer too."

Callie dropped her gaze, scrutinizing an ant busy hauling a berry. When was the last time she'd felt close to God? *The yellow rose.* God had spoken to her then in a message so eloquent that she'd locked the door on her past and come a thousand miles to follow his leading.

"Thank you for the way you handled Daniel last night." Marc's abrupt change of topic caused Callie to start.

"He's a wonderful little boy."

"My sister is so focused on her own problems she's missing the joy of her son's childhood." His candid comment caught Callie by surprise. "I'm glad you're here, Callie. Not only for the musical, but for Daniel's sake too."

"Rachael will be all right," Callie offered, understanding Marc's deep concern for her.

"I pray you're correct. But you see she doesn't have Christ to lean on. And without that resource, I don't think she's strong enough. I know I wasn't."

Callie opened her mouth to speak, but realized she had

nothing to say. Her own testimony wasn't very worthy. A frown creased Marc's forehead, and she wanted to reach up and smooth it away. But she couldn't. She was his business partner. They had work to do. And once the job was done, they'd go their separate ways. She'd leave behind Marc and Rachael and Daniel for good. She couldn't afford to get too involved because she didn't think she'd ever be strong enough to survive the loss of one more thing she loved.

Callie was amazed at how quickly she and Marc established their work routine. Both early risers, they talked first thing in the morning, outlining the Book of Acts and choosing scenes and incidents they wanted to build songs around. They broke for breakfast at eight, joining Rachael and Daniel, then went back to their work, stopping only when Mrs. Kaufman brought sandwiches and soup, amid admonishments of how their "eyes would fall out with all this work and no food."

They worked through the afternoon, until four, when Callie went into the kitchen to be with Daniel as he snacked on cookies and milk. Soon, their afternoons together became a ritual the boy looked to eagerly. Even Callie found them a welcome interlude after hours of struggling with melodies that didn't quite sing and words that didn't say what she wanted. After supper, she and Marc returned to the music room, where they rehashed the day's work. At eleven Marc would lower the cover over the piano keys, massage Callie's tired shoulders, and walk her up to her room. By the end of the second week, Callie had been lulled into a sense of purpose and contentment.

The only thing out of sync in the household was

Rachael. She was restless and agitated. She ate little, acted shrewish, almost ignored her son. She often dressed and drove off in her sports car to the city night life. Sometimes Callie heard Marc arguing with his sister, but Rachael seemed bent on self-destruction. Callie attempted to make it up to Daniel, unsure of why she felt she should, knowing only that she must.

"What do you think of this dress, Callie?" Rachael asked one evening, twirling in a slinky sequined sheath that covered her like a second skin. The dress was slit up one side, exposing the length of her leg, from ankle to thigh.

"It's–uh–bold."

"You don't approve of little Rachael either, do you, Callie?"

Callie shrugged. "You're my friend, Rachael. You have so much, yet you're so unhappy. It shows."

"You sound like Marc," Her voice sounded bitter. She crossed the living room and picked up a sequined handbag. "Have you any idea what it's like to grow up with all this, Callie?" She gestured grandly and when Callie said nothing, Rachael continued. "Do you know what it's like being the pampered Jewish princess, wanting for nothing . . . except to be like everybody else?

"I was a Rothstein you see. Not just another of the Long Island wealthy, but a person apart, a Jew. I went to Jewish schools, had only Jewish friends, lived according to Jewish customs. Every year, Father decorated Rothstein's in the finest Christmas decorations money could buy. I saw my Christian acquaintances buying and giving gifts. I'd ask father, 'Why can't we have a Christmas tree?' He'd say—as if I'd wounded him—'Rachael! We're Jewish. We celebrate

Chanukah.' It all seemed so hypocritical to me. Decorations and trees and nativity scenes for the store, but at home . . ." She blinked, as if to turn off the memory.

"I didn't want to celebrate Christmas really. I–I just wanted to touch the joy I saw in some of those people who did celebrate it. My Jewishness set me apart. I felt lonely, cut off. And the only thing I ever did on my own—marry Richard and give birth to Daniel—I botched."

"But you love Daniel—"

"Of course I do." Her mouth twisted in a bittersweet smile. "He's all I have now. But I don't look to him for happiness." She cocked her head, her gaze turning quizzical. "Are *you* happy, Callie? Does being 'Christian' make you happy?"

Rachael's question pricked. Callie bristled. "I know what it's like to lose people you love. I know that keeping busy, running around, and doing 'things' doesn't always make the pain go away. I know that loneliness is not unique to either the Jew or Christian."

The two women regarded each other warily, eye to eye, across the distance of the room. "Aren't we the pair, Callie? Me trying to catch the brass ring . . . you trying to let go of it. At least I know that I'm missing something. If I had a fraction of what you do, I'd count myself the most fortunate woman in the universe."

Callie stepped backward, confused and uncertain by the direction of the conversation. "I don't know what you're talking about."

Rachael gave a sad, rueful smile. "I know you don't. 'There's none so blind as she who will not see,' " she quoted. She grasped the door knob and added, "Would you please tuck Daniel in for me? I won't be home until very late."

Callie watched stupified as Rachael left. Panic welled inside her and she shivered. *Blind? How am I blind?* Confusion came, pushing aside Rachael's comments. Where was the peace and sense of purpose she'd gotten off the plane with? Where was the surety that she was doing God's will she'd felt so keenly only weeks before? She hurried to find Marc, knowing that although she wouldn't tell him of her and Rachael's conversation, she needed his presence to stop the cold, hard fear that gripped her.

"We did some good stuff yesterday," Marc said lazily, above the persistent buzz of a circling honeybee. April had blended into May and their mornings together were renewal for Callie's soul. His company, his quiet words, and his soft green eyes became the fuel that fired her creative juices. What was she going to do without him . . . when the project was over?

"Yes, we did, didn't we."

"Don't get smug."

Playfully, she stuck out her tongue at him. He leaned over and tapped the tip of her nose with his finger, allowing his hand to hold her chin and his thumb to rub intimately against the corner of her mouth. "Naughty girl." He was so close, Callie could see the sunshine reflect off his pupils. She fought a stab of emotional panic, struggled to break his spell over her.

Marc drew away, angry with himself. He'd pushed her again. He'd touched her in a too-intimate way. Not even when he kneaded her shoulders at night was the action anything but routine. Yet this morning, he'd gotten too close. Hunger to taste her mouth surged through him. He wanted to smash down her walls, pull her to him, and take his fill of her lips. His hands clenched involuntarily, restraining him from taking what he so desperately wanted.

Callie lowered her defenses, tempted to lean into him, nestle against his chest. Rachael burst out into the garden at just that moment. Unmindful of Callie, Rachael headed straight for her brother.

"He's gone too far this time, Marc! You've got to do something!"

"Slow down. What's going on?"

"It's Uncle Sol. Elaine just told me that he's officially named that wimpy husband of hers acting president of Rothstein's. How could he do that, Marc? He knows Father wanted Daniel to have the store." Rachael paced, fuming, sputtering with anger.

"Calm down." Marc rose and took his sister's arm. "Be practical. Daniel's only a child. Someone has to run the store until he can."

Rachael spat, "By that time, Murray will be a fixture. We won't be able to blast him out with dynamite. Sol should have appointed a board to oversee things until Daniel grows up. . . ." She wrenched free of Marc's hold.

"What else?"

"Aunt Barrie and Elaine—my *dear* aunt and cousin," Rachael almost gagged over the words. "They suggested that I might want to let Elaine and Murray have this house. After all, the president of Rothstein's should live here. What could a divorcee and one small boy do with such a big, monstrous house . . . ?" Her voice choked with emotion as she related their conversation in a sing-song litany.

Callie saw Marc recoil, his wrath boiling beneath a forced calm façade as he stroked his sister's hair. His green eyes had grown dark and hard, like emerald ice. "I think it's time we had Uncle Sol and his family over for dinner, Rachael. Tell Mrs. Kaufman to plan something special for Wednesday night. We'll eat at eight, after Daniel goes to bed."

Rachael peered up at him, clinging to him like a drowning person to a life preserver. "Thank you, Marc. I knew you'd help me."

"Perhaps, I should plan to eat in my room— " A brutal glance from Marc broke off Callie's words.

"You'll dine with us," he said. "As long as you're under this roof, you're a part of this family, Callie. And it's about time we Christians faced the lions together."

The tension at the dinner table that Wednesday night was as thick as coastland fog off Long Island Sound. Marc sat at the head of the table, dominant, almost princely in a grey worsted suit and ivory-colored silk foulard tie. He carved the turkey expertly, forcing those seated at the table to focus on the flash of his steel carving knives. Long candles burned in silver candelabras, glancing glints of fire off the sharpened blades.

Callie surveyed the entourage. Uncle Sol sat stiffly, dressed in a mortician's black shark-skin suit that matched his eyes. Aunt Barrie, a plump, matronly woman adorned in rose-colored voile and smelling of lavender, kept her hands folded in her lap. Elaine, slim and almost arrogant in red satin, eyed her cousin Marc with open hostility. Murray, a thin man with pale skin and a prematurely balding head, stared, mesmerized by Marc's agile display of cutlery skill. Rachael's eyes kept darting around the table, while tight lines around her mouth betrayed her strain.

Nostalgically Callie remembered meals at the Hansons' dining room table, recalled the laughter and love emanating from that family. Neither of those accompanied this dinner. This was a power struggle, a battle in the undeclared war between uncle and nephew. Silently, Callie uttered a prayer of support for Marc.

"Rachael tells me Elaine and Murray want this house."

"I never said—" Elaine started to explain.

Marc silenced her with a look. "I'm talking to your father, Elaine."

Sol's eyes didn't waver from Marc's face. "It was a gesture of goodwill. I thought perhaps Rachael and Daniel might enjoy something smaller, a bit more homey."

"Father wanted his grandson raised in this house. Just as he wanted him to take over Rothstein's some day."

Nervously, Murray cleared his throat. "I'm merely a temporary president. I won't do anything to endanger Daniel's inheritance."

Marc shot him a withering glance. "I know who runs the store, Murray." He fixed his green eyes on Sol. "I only want to make very sure Rachael is left in peace to raise her son. And she wants to raise him in this house to take over his grandfather's store."

"Marc, you'll be leaving to go back to your career soon. Rachael's a major stockholder. Over time, there will be decisions to make. Someone will have to look out for

Daniel and Rachael's interest—" Sol got no further. Marc carefully laid the carving knives on the platter and impaled his uncle with a glare.

"*I* will be looking out for Rachael's interests. I have general power-of-attorney and nothing can be done on her behalf unless I okay it."

Elaine gasped audibly. Sol's lips drew into a tight, narrow line. "Is this true, Rachael? Did you give him *carte blanche* over all your affairs? Your income?"

Rachael pressed the tips of her fingers together. "I did."

Sol whirled toward Marc. "Who do you think you are?"

"I'm her brother and my father's son—"

"Your father disowned you! He wanted nothing to do with you. It was you who spit on your heritage . . . abandoned your family . . ."

Callie saw Marc flinch, but he did not look away. His words came with deliberation. "I wonder how the New York court feels about a will written by some old Jew who tore his clothes and disowned his only son?"

Aunt Barrie's hand flew to cover her mouth to stifle a cry. Uncle Sol blanched. "Are you telling me you'd stoop to contesting your father's will? That you'd fight in court for Rothstein's?"

Callie arched an eyebrow, her heart hammering. What cat and mouse game was Marc playing with his uncle? She knew he didn't want the department store.

"I will do whatever necessary to save my sister from her 'well-intentioned' relatives."

"You'd never win!" Sol rasped.

"Maybe . . ." Marc drew out the word. "But it might take years to be settled. And it would be very messy. The newspapers would have a heyday."

Sol stood and leaned forward, braced by his knuckles on the table. "Don't threaten me, Marc."

"I don't threaten, Uncle Sol. I make promises."

The room grew quiet as the two men locked wills. A dollop of wax from a candle plopped onto the lace tablecloth. The turkey seemed suddenly unappetizing, vulnerable and naked, a half-carved carcass.

Sol straightened, his complexion white, pasty, his black eyes sullen and hostile. "Come on, Barrie." He threw his linen napkin onto his plate. "We won't stay in a house where we're not wanted."

The foursome stood in unison. Callie was the only one left sitting, and she felt dwarfed. Rachael quickly edged next to Marc, a look of triumph on her face. "As my father's brother you will always be welcome in this house, Uncle Sol." Marc's tone had softened. "As will all your family. But I make the rules now. All I ask is that you honor them."

Stiffly, awkwardly, the gathering shuffled from the dining room, toward the front door. Callie followed, hesitant, hanging in the background. In the living room, Marc paused. Obediently, the group jerked to a halt as he studiously contemplated the room as if seeing it through new eyes. The furniture looked dingy, aged, part of a stuffy and constricting past. "Uncle Sol . . . tomorrow I want you to send out the best decorator on Rothstein's payroll. Since this house now belongs to Rachael, I think it should reflect its present mistress."

Sol opened his mouth to speak, thought better of it, and gave a brusque nod. At the door, Marc called to his uncle again. "And would you please do me one more favor? Have the best landscape architect in New York sent out too. I want my mother's gardens to bloom again."

"As you wish," Uncle Sol's tone was as tight as a bow string.

The group evaporated into the humid night, in cars that vanished like Victorian coaches down the lantern-lit driveway. Marc shut the massive doors, walked into the living room and stood staring out into the blackness through an open curtain, his hands clasped behind his back. Callie fought the urge to go to him, touch him. She slowly climbed the stairs, leaving the silent brooding man alone in the corridors of his thoughts.

chapter 9

"RACHAEL, I DON'T UNDERSTAND what you're telling me. What do you mean you want to go 'away for a while'?" Marc was seated at the piano where he and Callie had been working before Rachael had invaded their territory and made her request.

"It's not very hard to figure out, Marc. I'm exhausted. I need to go away, take a break, get some rest." The petite woman appeared as an ideal picture for her case. The dark circles under her eyes, the gauntness of her cheeks, made her look wraithlike.

Marc shook his head. "What about redecorating this house? I thought you were working with the woman from the store—"

Rachael interrupted. "What's to work with? She shows me some samples and swatches. I pick out wallpaper from a book, material and carpet samples . . . it's not very challenging you know. Any moron could do it."

"You have a son, Rachael. Daniel needs you."

"Don't start plying me with guilt! I know my responsibilities. Good grief, Marc! I'm thirty-one years old, and I still can't do things for myself. When is it my turn? When do I get the opportunity to be myself?" Rachael turned to Callie, who observed the interplay, sheets of music spread in front of her on a work desk. "Callie, can't you help me? Can't you make him understand?"

"Rachael . . . I—"

"Oh, never mind! I should have realized that I'm still a prisoner in this house. That I'll never have a life of my own!" Rachael turned, fled to the door and jerked it open. Callie and Marc listened as the double doors of the sound lock slammed behind her retreat.

"I think she's cross," Marc muttered dryly.

"She's also right."

"So you're on her side?"

"I'm not taking sides. But I can verify that if Farrell Hanson had not dragged me to Michigan, forced me to leave the past behind—well, I'm not sure I would have kept my sanity."

Marc listened to her words with his inner ear, knowing that exposure of past hurts was difficult for her. "I hear what you're saying, Callie. But Rachael's so different from you. She has no anchor, no foundation. She's running away *from,* not *toward* something. And she certainly doesn't exercise good sense."

Callie crossed her arms over her chest, a defensively motion. She'd not meant to talk about herself. "No, Rachael isn't sensible. But she's hurting. Do you remember the story in the Bible about the son who demanded his inheritance and the father who gave it to him, knowing that the boy would only go off and squander it?"

"The Parable of the Prodigal Son. Yes, I've read it many times."

"I think the father had to let the boy find out about himself on his own. Self-revelation is what makes people grow up."

Marc gazed down on her lovely upturned face. Impulsively, he twisted a curl around his finger. "What about Daniel?"

"I lo– like Daniel," Callie wished she could back away from Marc, but her perverse senses wanted her to press nearer. How could the touch of his hand unnerve her so? "Can't we fill in a while for Rachael? We can rearrange our work schedule and spend the early part of each evening with him. I don't mind working a little later every night. Besides, our work's going very well. Don't you think?"

Marc could deny Callie nothing. If his crazy sister needed some time to herself, then let her go. He dipped his mouth and brushed Callie lightly across her lips.

She started, disturbed not so much by his impulsive gesture as by her own desire to throw her arms around him.

"Okay, Callie. I'll send the prodigal sister off on a journey. And we'll stand in for her with her son. I think it's a mistake, but you're right, growing up requires self-revelation. She not getting it here." He locked elbows with her. "Let's go tell her to pick some place with interesting postcards—and for all our sakes let's make certain Mrs. Kaufman knows there'll be one less mouth to feed at mealtimes."

For the first few days after his mother left, Daniel was inconsolable. He cried, threw temper tantrums, and sulked. But gradually, Callie drew him out. "He feels deserted,"

Marc commented darkly. "First, his grandfather . . . now his mother."

"Then it's our job to make him feel wanted," Callie countered.

"A child can't differentiate between death and a vacation. Either way, he's lost someone he loves."

"We'll make it up to him, Marc. We will." The determination in her voice gave Marc pause to ponder its origin.

They settled into a new routine, starting the day early, but stopping to have lunch with Daniel in the music room and supper as a threesome in the dining room. After supper they played a game with Daniel, watched an hour of TV with him, then put him to bed, and went back to the music room. On Saturdays, Mrs. Kaufman took Daniel to the synagogue while Marc and Callie worked. On Sundays, Marc and Callie visited various area churches, slipping in and out to worship, but never to linger. Marc avoided recognition scrupulously. The pattern continued for a month, lulling Callie into an idyllic peace.

For Marc, the days were more difficult, and the nights almost impossible. Seeing her everyday, touching her, but not holding her, taxed his vow not to pressure her into an emotional confrontation with him. He realized he loved her, but she avoided entanglements, separating their professional and personal lives as adroitly as a dancer on a waxed stage.

He had been right about their collaboration; they were a brilliant team. He found her ability innate with a keen sensitivity to his own musical sense, complementing it, reinforcing it. They argued, sometimes hotly, over specifics, but always came away with powerful, perfected music. The score took shape, the songs had substance. It was good, and Marc knew it. Yes, Callie O'Ryan was the perfect foil to his creativity, yet he couldn't get inside her no matter what tack he took. Her dedication to the project, their music, was all she'd give him.

They met each morning in the garden, which was regaining its former splendor under the masterful touch of a Japanese gardener, who planted, watered, weeded, and reconstructed the dormant flowerbeds. Slowly, the plot blossomed to life, vibrant with color, alive with irises, jonquils, daisies, roses, box myrtle, and summer phlox. Often, Daniel joined them, pushing a toy dump truck across the flagstones, filling it with freshly turned earth, making grinding sounds in his throat.

Marc caught Callie watching Daniel one morning, some strange, undefinable emotion on her face. "Mr. Yomoto will appreciate your help in redistributing the dirt in the flowerbeds, Daniel." His voice held tender humor.

"I like it out here. It's pretty. It smells pretty too. Daniel turned to peer up at Callie, sitting next to Marc on the bench. "It smells like you sometimes, Aunt Callie."

"My perfume," She felt her face flush as Marc leaned over, lifted her hair and nuzzled her neck.

"You're right, Daniel. Callie smells just like the garden."

"Stop it, you two."

Marc's eyes danced mischievously. "You could drive a man crazy smelling that way, Callie."

"Are you crazy, Uncle Marc?"

"Insane," he confessed, pinning Callie with a look.

She felt the uncontrolled flutterings of her pulse and

commanded herself not to react to him. "Insane is right." She turned his words to another meaning and shoved him playfully.

He caught her wrist. " 'There once was a girl who had a little curl right in the middle of her forehead—' "

Daniel leaped up squealing, "I know the rest! She was horrid!"

"I can tell when I'm being ganged up on." Callie attempted to stand, but Daniel hurled himself at her knees. She fell backward and only Marc's arms prevented her from hitting the cement.

"What have we here?" Marc held her tightly. "A damsel in distress?"

The three of them ended up in a heap, hugging, laughing, tickling. Only the arrival of Mrs. Kaufman announcing breakfast saved Callie from a severe case of laughing hiccups. The woman tapped her foot, giving them all a stern look of admonishment. "What's this? I haven't enough to do that I need to referee you three? It's barely eight o'clock, and you're out here acting like wild children." She clucked her tongue, but Callie saw a softness in her eyes.

Marc shrugged. "I was minding my own business, and these two pests attacked me."

"Not true!" Callie countered. "Daniel and I were minding our own business. Isn't that right, Daniel?"

"He started it." Daniel pointed a finger at Marc.

"Well, I'm finishing it," Mrs. Kaufman announced. "Breakfast is getting cold. Which would you like? Scrambled eggs or oatmeal. I made both."

"Eggs for me," Marc said.

Mrs. Kaufman turned to him, a pained look on her face. "So what's the matter? You don't like my oatmeal?"

Callie got another attack of giggles watching Marc shake his head, an expression of 'can't win for losing' crossing his face. "I'll take both," Callie sniffed smugly.

"Such a smart girl," Mrs. Kaufman said with an indulgent smile. "See? Now there's a girl who knows how to start her day right."

The four of them swept into the house, and it hit Callie that she hadn't felt so much at home in years. She tried to feel guilty about finding such pleasure in Marc's life, but for this particular morning she couldn't force herself to feel anything but genuine contentment.

By mid-July, the musical was more than half-finished, and Marc told Alex to expect it to be completed by August. That meant a director could be hired, casting could be done, choreography designed, rehearsals started, and an opening off-Broadway date set for spring. If it were any good at all, it might cross over to "the Great White Way." This was Marc's goal, his ultimate dream . . . to have a Christian musical play to Broadway.

"I can't make anything work today, Marc." Callie was dejected. For some reason, her music had dried up. She tossed her pencil down on the pile of music pages and propped her elbows under her chin, emitting an exasperated sigh. "Maybe I have spring fever. . . ."

"It's the middle of July—a bit late for spring, don't you think?" He stared at her then, seeing the frustration in her face. His tone softened, and he put his guitar down on the floor next to his feet. "We're just tired. I think we're so close to finishing it, we're forcing it. We need a break." He stood and stretched, his T-shirt riding up over the band of his jeans, exposing his tight stomach muscles.

Callie glanced away. "So how do we get the 'magic' back?"

Marc's eyes sparkled with sudden inspiration. "How'd you like to go to the zoo?"

"Are you kidding? I taught music theory to college freshmen. I *lived* in a zoo."

"I was thinking of the New York City Zoo in Central Park. Daniel would love it."

Callie bounded up. "Could we?"

Her bubbling enthusiasm buoyed Marc's sagging energies. "We'll buy red hots and popcorn and cotton candy. . . ."

"Is it kosher?"

"We won't tell Mrs. Kaufman. Now, come on before I lose my nerve about overfeeding my nephew and making him sick to his stomach again."

Central Park brimmed with summer activity. A band played to a sparse audience near the lake while hansom cabs plodded lazily along the winding trails. Park benches were crowded with elderly women, their upturned, sunning faces resembling pastel flowers. Pigeons scooted from under pedestrians' feet and children spilled across green grass like animated toys. It was a day drowned in sunshine, decorated with blue sky and puffy clouds, smelling heavily of freshly cut grass and moisture-ladened air. Callie knew she would remember it always, bringing it out like a treasure from a box in years to come.

Daniel was wide-eyed, clinging to Callie and Marc's

hands, pulling them from cage to cage in the sprawling zoo. He pointed to the pandas and asked solemnly, "Why are they wearing masks?"

"It's just the way God made them," Marc explained.

At the penguins, Daniel stood for a full half-hour, staring in fascination at the waddling, formally attired birds as they slipped into the arctic water on their stomachs. At the snakehouse, he cowered behind his uncle's legs in front of the twelve-foot-long boa constrictor.

Marc kept up a running commentary on the various animals, but he never took his attention from Callie. She had become a different person, carefree and as childlike as Daniel, hovering over the boy, sharing his giggles and candy apples. Once, the red crusty sugar stuck to the corner of her mouth. Marc wiped it away with a dampened edge of his handkerchief. Their eyes locked and held, and only Daniel squealing for a drink pried them apart.

Callie felt a sense of freedom, of joy and abandon. She couldn't remember a time of such unparalleled bliss. What was it? Why did every moment in time become a jewel, crystallized by the sunshine and the contentment she felt with Marc and Daniel? It was as if God had opened the portals of heaven and rained happiness on her. She wanted to stop time, relive each minute of the day over and over. No one recognized Marc. Perhaps it was the setting—the zoo, a woman, a child, a summer day—but no one bothered him. Callie counted his anonymity a blessing. *Normal.* For the first time in years, she felt normal, comfortable, part of a whole.

During the late afternoon Callie stood watching Daniel and Marc ride atop a lumbering old circus elephant, bedecked with a Rajah's canopy. Next to her, an elderly lady commented, "Your family's lovely."

"Oh, but they're not— I mean, thank you." *My family*. It struck her like a thunderbolt. To everyone who saw them, they appeared to be a family.

"The boy looks like his father," the woman beamed. "Except for the color of his eyes."

His uncle . . . the words of correction stuck in Callie's throat. "Yes, he does. . . ."

"I'll bet he gets his smile from your side of the family. Such a handsome child."

I'm not his mother . . . "He has a wonderful smile."

"Well, ride's finished." The woman patted Callie's arm. "God bless you and your little family, dear." Callie stared after her blankly while she vanished into the swelling crowds. A cloud passed over the sun, casting grayness across the day.

"Did you see me, Aunt Callie? Did you see me ride the elephant just like Tarzan?" Daniel tugged at the cuff of her white Bermuda shorts. She touched the child's cheek, pushing down some cold, hard tide that had risen within her.

"Are you all right, Callie?" Marc's tone was quizzical. "You look pale. Don't tell me you've had too much cotton candy and have a tummy ache."

She forced a smile. "Things are never what they seem." Her comment was cryptic and lost on Marc.

"I pretended that I was gonna rescue Jane and Cheeta," Daniel continued.

Pretending. Callie knew all about pretending. How had she allowed this to happen? How had she allowed herself to become so involved with Marc and Daniel and Rachael? After all her stern warnings to herself, she'd rushed headlong into an impossible relationship. *Stupid! Foolish and very stupid.* She scrambled internally for the emotional security of distance between herself and Marc. "I think I've had enough fun, Marc. Do you suppose we could call it a day and head ho– back to the house." She corrected herself just in time. She had no home.

Marc watched helplessly, as Callie slipped away from him. Bewilderment, then anger gripped him. What had gone wrong? What had transpired in Callie's mind during the ten minutes it had taken to ride an elephant? "Of course. If you're ready, we can leave now."

"Do we have to, Uncle Marc?" Daniel wailed.

"The party's over, kid." Marc pointed his words like darts, tousled the boy's hair, lifted him to his shoulders, and led the way out of the zoo.

"Did you have a good time today?" Marc chose the sentence carefully, constructing it in his mind minutes before he asked it.

Callie sat on the sofa of the music workroom, pouring over pages of handwritten notes. "A fine time. We certainly wore Daniel out. He was asleep before his head hit the pillow."

"Callie, look at me." Slowly, she raised her eyes. "What's wrong?"

"Nothing. I'm on a streak. I feel a 'song coming on,'" she said with forced gaiety.

He took the pencil from her hands and pulled her to her feet. "I asked you once to trust me. Talk to me, Callie. Tell me what's on your mind."

Her heart began to pound crazily. Her hands felt cold. *I'm a liar. I let a woman believe that you and Daniel were mine.* "I'm going up to bed now." She pulled away. He made a move to follow. "I can make it up the stairs by myself."

Marc stiffened. He watched her leave—more accurately—flee, impotent with frustration. Why? Why?

Callie stopped at the far side of the double-door sound lock, trembling, struggling to regain her composure. What was happening to her? Why was she acting this way? Marc deserved better. Much better. *Marc . . . Marc . . .* Her pulse hammered his name. Behind her, she heard him pounding the piano keys. The notes chased her through the empty house and up the stairs, relentless, demanding, sounding wild and hurt and angry.

A child was crying. From far away, Callie could hear him sobbing. In her dream, she kept trying to find him, twisting through long, dark tunnels, mutely struggling to locate and comfort him. She awoke with a start, alert, snapped from the dream by a wailing noise. A child *was* crying. Daniel! She jumped from her bed and hurried down the hall to his room.

"Honey . . . it's all right, I'm here. What's the matter?" She settle on his bed and smoothed his hair from his damp forehead.

"The m–monster was c–chasing me . . . It was a big snake. This long." He gestured with his arms, spanning the expanse of his narrow bed.

Callie kissed his cheek and nestled him closer. The dim aura from his nightlight cast his features in soft shadow.

She saw the fear in his eyes. "It was only a bad dream, honey."

"I–I'm s–scared."

"You're safe in your very own room, in your very own bed. Nothing can harm you. Tell you what . . . why don't I sit with you until you fall asleep."

"You won't go away?" He clutched at her as she shifted.

"Not until you're fast asleep."

He held her hand, stretched stiffly beneath his covers and stared up at his ceiling. Sleep tugged at his eyes, despite his struggle to keep them open. Callie flipped his hair. She saw the shape of the square Rothstein jawline, and traced it tenderly. "Mama . . . ," the boy murmured.

Her hand froze. "No, Daniel," she said very deliberately. "It's Aunt Callie . . . not Mama."

His lashes fluttered open, and he twisted his head fiercely on the pillow. "No! I want you to be my Mama. Daniel's Mama."

Ghosts . . . phantoms, came for her. Callie recoiled, desperate to get out of their way. *A doctor's voice from long ago said, "You're a healthy young woman, Mrs. O'Ryan. You'll have other children."*

The rhythmic flow of Daniel's breathing signaled that he was asleep. Shakily, Callie stood, leaned down, and kissed his cheek. *Cold. Why am I so cold?* She turned toward the door and stopped, stark still. Marc was there. Framed in the door, clad in his pajama bottoms, his torso bare. How long had he been watching? She tried to step around him. "Daniel had a bad dream. . . ."

"You're ice cold." He took her hand and led her down the hall, back to her room. He flipped on a bedside lamp and stroked the tangled mass of her hair. He wanted to rip apart barehanded the demons that were tearing at her. If only he could get her to talk to him, tell him . . . "Callie . . . Daniel's fine now."

"He called me 'Mama'." Her voice was a whisper.

Marc tipped her chin up and trailed his gaze over her features, searching for some clue, some small chink in her wall. "He was confused, scared. By tomorrow morning he won't remember a thing. He's only four years old."

"My baby would have been four years old too."

Her words landed in his gut like lead. *Her baby . . . What baby?* "I–I didn't know. . . ."

She nestled against Marc, wrapping her arms across the smooth, muscular expanse of his back, sagging against the lean hardness of his chest. The soft mat of hair on his chest rubbed against her cheek. She listened to the beating of his heart. "I miscarried the day of Kevin's funeral. I couldn't even hold on to his baby. First, Kevin. Then the baby. I have a problem holding onto the things I love. Why do you suppose that is?"

Marc had no answers. He tried to absorb her hurts, to soak them into himself and shield her from the complexity of a past he'd had no part of. "Callie . . ."

The whispered sound of her name brought her back to the present. Marc's arms felt wonderful! Why had she not tried them before? She had wanted to . . . time and again. She nuzzled the thick hair of his chest and muttered, "It's all right. I'm all right. Really. I–I didn't even realize that I still thought about it." Her head cleared to the rising surge of her own pulse.

Marc sensed the change in her. Having confronted the

demons, she'd driven them out—at least for the time being. The touch of her breath on his bare skin had caused electricity to arc from his reason to his senses. With the possessive weight of her arms across his back, he felt a sliver of desire prickling up his spine. It prodded devilishly at his will power. He cupped her chin in his palm. In the dim lamplight, her lashes looked soft, like luxurious mink, and her eyes became warm pools of golden honey. He got stuck in them. His hand caressed her jaw, and slowly he lowered his mouth to hers.

At the touch of his mouth, fire blazed within her. She tightened her hold, running her palms up his back to touch the nape of his neck and twine her fingers in his hair. *Marc . . . Marc* . . . Every cell in her body screamed his name. She was lost in him, trapped in a tapestry of taste and texture and warmth.

Her need for him was alive, and Marc knew it. Hunger, sharp as a dagger, tore through his insides—white hot, consuming. He broke their kiss, anxious to side-step the vortex threatening to engulf them.

Callie sucked in her breath. She felt soft, liquid. "Stay with me, Marc. Please . . . just for tonight. Don't leave me alone . . . stay with me."

The desire of his heart. To stay with her, make love to her . . . Hadn't that been what he'd wanted from the first time he'd met her? Hadn't that been his goal when he'd lured her into his life months before? He searched her face, probing into her very soul with his hot green eyes. Unbidden memories from his own past rose up to mock him. *Marc Raphael . . . Superstar* . . . He'd once had anything . . . and anyone he'd wanted. He wanted more with Callie. Suddenly he wanted everything with her. Commitment. Physical and spiritual union. His voice took on fervency. "Callie, listen to me. I can't take you in bits and pieces. A night here, a few hours there. I need more from you."

Fear froze her, quenching the fire of passion. She tensed, took a step backward. *No. That isn't possible.* Commitment meant trusting, giving, and she wasn't ready for that, wasn't ready to lose again. In her mind the equation was very simple. Callie loves. Callie loses. She refused to walk down that road, to face the inevitability of having the people she loved torn out of her life time after time. Marc Raphael was fantasy. He always had been.

Marc helplessly watched her slip away from him, unable to stop her slide into isolation. She pulled out of his embrace, turned her back, hugged her arms to herself. "It's late. I should go to bed. We have work to do tomorrow. . . ."

He almost changed his mind, picked her up, and carried her to the big four-poster bed. He balanced between the two choices. Yet finally, he left the room and shut the door, fighting the urge to splinter it with his fist. He'd gambled and lost. He'd asked her for more of herself than she could relinquish. The bitter taste of defeat filled his mouth. He'd lost. Marc leaned momentarily against the surface of the wall, breathing in gulps of air, feeling as if he'd been pummeled in the stomach by a giant's fist. He'd lost. Marc uttered an oath, the first he'd used since his days with the band, then went downstairs into the darkened maw of the music room.

Callie rolled into a tight ball, clutching the covers up to her neck. What had she done? Dear God . . . what had she done? She'd all but begged Marc to make love to her! Shame and humiliation coursed through her. He'd refused. Wisely, he'd turned her down. Oh, his rejection had been gentle, couched in words of wanting more than a one-night stand, but Callie understood perfectly well what he had meant. She was no better than any of the silly teenage girls who flung themselves at him during his days as a rock star.

What must Marc think of her? What must God think of her? She silently begged forgiveness from her Creator. That was the easy part. God was faceless, an ethereal Spirit. But Marc? Marc Raphael was flesh and blood. In the morning she'd go to him, ask his forgiveness too. Yes . . . there was no other recourse. They still had to complete the musical. *Not much longer* she told herself. *Soon it will be complete.* Then she could get out of his life and back to the safety of . . . of what?

chapter 10

THROUGHOUT THE LONG NIGHT, Callie replayed the scenes from the previous day in her mind like a bad movie. From the woman at the zoo who mistook Marc and Daniel for Callie's family, to Daniel's dream, to the emotional upheaval of her past to Marc, to the sensuous delight she'd felt in his arms. The journey had been progressional, each incident building and leading into the other. The things she felt for Marc, those feelings she'd repressed and ignored all during the past months, had clawed their way out, erupting into her brazen display in his arms. *"Stay with me, Marc. Just for tonight . . ."* Her words hounded her, stealing sleep.

At seven, Callie tossed off the covers and showered, letting the needle-fine water stab through the fog of too little rest and too long a night. She dressed mechanically, choosing linen slacks of mahogany brown and a cotton baggy shirt of warm bronze. She tied back her red-blond hair with a brown grosgrain ribbon, applied her make-up, and headed down to the garden to do what she knew she must.

Marc sat in his usual spot on the familiar bench,

silhouetted by a lacy filigree of golden-yellow forsythia. He stood when he heard her coming. They appraised one another for a few moments, Marc guarded, wary; Callie, nervous, feeling anew the sting of shame. "Good morning."

A smile flicked at the corner of his mouth. "At least you *look* like you slept better than I did."

She attempted a smile. He was making it easy for her so she decided to get the apology said as quickly as possible. "Marc, please forgive me for last night. I acted very foolish and jeopardized our working relationship. I–I don't want to do anything to hurt the project."

The tilt of her head warned him that she'd rehearsed her speech carefully. "There's nothing to forgive, Callie."

"I–I all but threw myself at you. . . . If you'd been less the man you are . . ." Her cheeks burned. In the bright light of day, her actions were even more humiliating.

Her self-loathing rankled him. Marc couldn't stand for her to think she was to blame, that he hadn't wanted her in his bed for months. He took her by the shoulders, his strong fingers digging through the thin material of her shirt. "Listen to me, Callie . . . I find you a very desirable woman. Make no mistake, I wanted to stay. God help me, I wanted to stay. So don't go pinning on me badges of nobility that I don't deserve."

"Don't be kind. As Marc Raphael, I know that women have thrown themselves at you for years. I never wanted to be like all the rest. . . ."

Her words stung. "Why can't you believe that you are different? You'll never be like any of the others. I'm not proud of the life I used to lead, or of the man I used to be. I used people. Oh, they often made it easy for me—wanting so much to be a part of my lifestyle, but that doesn't excuse the way I treated them."

"Sometimes, I'd wake up and not even be able to remember the name of the woman next to me. Do you know how disgusting that is? When I became a Christian, I couldn't live that way any more. I had to put on 'the new man.' That meant leaving a very strong-willed, self-gratifying 'old man' behind."

She hooked her hands over his wrists resting on her shoulders and stared into the tortured windows of his eyes. She'd hurt him! With one act of selfish need, she'd forced him to review things he'd spent years leaving behind. "I'm so sorry. I never meant to hurt you . . . compromise you. It was inexcusable."

He dropped his hands and dragged long fingers through his straight, dark hair. A sunshower glinted off the still-damp strands. "Callie, I believe that God forgets when he forgives. Often Christians don't forget or forgive themselves and that only serves to separate us from him and from each other. He forgave me for the man I once was . . . and, more important, I forgave myself."

Callie tensed as his words ricocheted off her psyche. What was Marc saying to her? How could he possibly know the guilt she'd felt over Kevin's death? Or the baby's? How did he know the innermost workings of her mind?

Absently, Marc reached out to twirl her hair around his forefinger in the gesture of familiarity he often used. "Some good did come out of it, Callie. You told me things about yourself you never had before. Thank you for that."

She jutted her jaw, suddenly anxious to keep him at

arm's length. "It–it didn't seem important that you should know anything more personal than what you already know. I mean, after all, we are really just business partners. All we truly have between us is the project."

Marc eyed her speculatively as she scurried into her cocoon of protection. "Yes, the project is very important, and we can't allow anything to break up that magic we have when we write music together." He paused, dug his hands into the pockets of his jeans and rocked backward on his heels. "But there won't always be a project between us, Callie. Sooner or later, the project will be finished."

Her large, luminous eyes turned to stare at him. "I know," she whispered, seeing her days without him stretch into an unbroken ribbon of loneliness. "I know."

The awkwardness vanished between them once they started work. Callie wrote a fast-paced, tongue-in-cheek number she called, "Taking Off the Old Man." She played it for Marc shyly, anxious to have their creative ebb and flow return to normal. He liked its humor and style, and the change of pace it added to the overall score. He flashed her a rueful smile of acceptance after he heard it for the first time.

He fashioned a love ballad named, "Shipwrecked Dreams," centered around Paul's experiences on his journey to Italy to face Caesar's court. The wistful, poignant melody brought the sting of tears to Callie's eyes. She thought it was the best number of the score.

Callie also concentrated on keeping herself emotionally aloof from Daniel. She assumed the attitude of professional teacher in all her dealings with him, talking to him about his mother at every opportunity. She helped him pin photos of his mother onto a bulletin board and helped him draw pictures to enclose in letters she wrote to Rachael. Rachael's own letters and cards were sporadic, the postmarks spanning the major cities of Europe.

"She needs to come home," Marc groused one evening. "She's been 'finding herself' long enough. But she's never in one place long enough for me to contact her and tell her."

"I'm sure she's doing fine," Callie countered, yet she too was uneasy about Rachael's lack of communication and failure to earmark a specific date for her return. "And she has to come home because she wants to, not because you order her to. Remember the prodigal son."

"She has more money than the prodigal son. Do you know how much the Rothstein inheritance is worth? It may take her years to come to her senses."

Callie chuckled. "Then pray for famine. Maybe she has to see a few pigpens before she thinks about home."

"Pigpens aren't kosher."

Callie tossed a pencil at him, but he ducked with a playful grin. "Get back to work," she ordered.

They went to church one Sunday—Marc, Callie, and Daniel. Mrs. Kaufman voiced her disapproval about taking the boy, but Marc insisted, saying, "He needs to know more than Judaism." They entered a small brick church building that claimed no denomination, choosing seats mid-center, near the red-carpeted aisle. Daniel twisted his neck to see over the backs of the pews and asked, "Why aren't we sitting on the front row, Uncle Marc? Grandpa always sat on the front row in synagogue."

To Callie Marc said, "The closer a Jew sits to the front, the more important his position in the congregation. Only the men who give very generously get to sit in the front row." To Daniel he said, "In this church people sit wherever they want. God looks at people's hearts, not their seating order."

"Well, where's the Rabbi? And why are the candles in those kinds of holders, and where's the *menorah?*"

Patiently, Marc explained that the rabbi in this "synagogue" was called a minister, and he was the man in the black suit, and that the seven-branched candelabrum wasn't used in this sanctuary.

"Where's the Eternal Light and the ark and the Torah?" the boy quizzed again.

At Callie's questioning look, Marc explained, "In the synagogue an oil lamp hangs in front of the ark, which is where the Torah—hand-lettered scrolls of the Books of Moses—rests." Marc pointed to the huge wooden cross hanging on the wall behind the pulpit area, "That's the ark of the new covenant, Daniel. Jesus Christ is the Eternal Light, and he came and fulfilled the Law, so the cross takes the place of the ark now."

When the organ music sounded, Daniel started another stream of questions. "Few synagogues have musical accompaniment," Marc clarified for Callie. "The cantor chants much of the service, usually in Hebrew." Daniel liked the resonant music, however, holding his hymnal upside down, staring at it studiously as if he could read the words. Callie turned her head to keep from laughing out loud at the boy's serious efforts to participate.

Daniel pointed to a stained-glass window that contained

a Star of David as part of its motif. "I know what that is," he exclaimed. But a white-robed Christ standing between a lion and a lamb caused him to ask, "Won't the lion eat up the sheep?"

"Not with Jesus, the Perfect Shepherd, watching over them," Marc assured the worried boy. Callie watched Daniel screw up his face, attempting to put it all together in his mind. "Was Jesus Jewish?"

"Yes. He is also the promised Messiah."

"Did the Messiah come already?" Daniel's voice held genuine surprise. "Why didn't Rabbi tell me about it?"

Marc tousled Daniel's hair. "Rabbi doesn't know."

"Someone should tell him. He's still waiting." The boy studied the minister intently as he preached. He asked no more questions, but Callie could sense the wheels turning inside his head. Marc had opened a door for the child. She wasn't sure how Rachael would react, but she was glad the seed had been sown and delighted that Marc Rothstein-Raphael had done it.

In mid-August, Janette Hanson called. "Callie?" Her voice crackled over the wire. "How are you? Have you forgotten your friends back in Michigan?"

Callie hugged the receiver and let lose a delighted bubble of laughter. "Never! How's everybody?"

"Farrell is wrapping up the summer term, and we're going to the Upper Peninsula for a three-week vacation. The girls are clamoring—" Callie heard Janette muffle the mouthpiece and say, "Calm down, Meli. I'll let you say hi in a minute."

Waves of homesickness swept through Callie, not for the

old lifestyle, but for her old friends. "Give everyone my love."

"We were wondering if you might be almost finished with that musical. If so, how'd you like to join us up at our lake place?"

How like Janette to think of Callie, to give her a option once her and Marc's work was finished. Because she'd been uncertain in the spring of how long the project would take, she'd taken a leave-of-absence from her teaching position. Her apartment was leased through the fall semester. She really didn't have any place to go once the musical was completed. And Callie desperately didn't want to be alone. "I–I hadn't thought about it. I guess I should."

"Er—how . . . are things going? I mean is working with Marc Raphael as wonderful as you thought it would be?"

"More."

"Might you be staying?"

"Of course not. Once the score's finished, my contract expires."

A short silence fell between them. "Well, remember our offer. The lake's beautiful this time of the year. And we'd love to have you."

"Thank you." Uncertainty grated like sandpaper against Callie's nerves. What was she going to do? Where was she going to go? She sighed and said with forced brightness, "Now let me speak to Meli before she bursts."

"You'll get back to me?"

"Yes. In a couple weeks." She spoke with Meli, said her good-bys and hung up the receiver deep in thought. The Hansons, Michigan, her job at the college . . . they all seemed a lifetime away. Marc Raphael had so filled her days that she could barely recall not having him near her. "It's got to change," she told herself in sharp tones of dismissal. Somehow, she had to break his invisible hold on her heart and make a new life for herself. Yet she also knew it would take all her will power to figure out just how.

Marc basked in the afternoon fragrance of the still garden, seeking again the comforting peace he always found there. Daily, the task became more difficult. Soon the musical would be complete, and Callie would feel obligated to leave. He didn't want that, but the bittersweet agony of having her so close and still so distant was taxing his sanity.

He knew that the Hansons had offered her a vacation with them, but he wasn't ready to let go of her yet. More time . . . he craved more time to persuade her that she needed him in her life. She'd been gun-shy, absolutely stoic since the night of their physical encounter. He wryly wondered if his own self-discipline would hold out much longer; yet to watch her go . . . to have her leave him . . . He strummed his guitar, pulling an occasional note into a vibrato that hung shimmering in the air and watched her covertly as she scribbled notes to herself on a yellow legal pad.

Callie sat cross-legged on the flagstones surrounded by an army of daisies and black-eyed Susans, feigning concentration on her notations and hearing instead the plaintive cords from Marc's classical guitar. Every note was a stab at the ache she felt inside whenever she thought about leaving. The pulsating notes tugged invisible strings in her heart. They called to her, beckoned . . .

It was Marc who finally spoke, breaking the current of tension in the warm summer stillness. "Callie . . . I've been thinking. . . . We'll be wrapping this up in another week or so. Have you thought about staying on and watching the production come to life?"

She jerked her head up, instantly focusing on his face, her heart thudding in her chest. "What can I do? I know nothing about producing a play."

"Alex and I are meeting with the producers after Labor Day. Even though they've named a director and choreographer, watching them cast the play and block it can be kind of fun. Have you ever been to a 'cattle call'?"

"I thought it was something they did out West."

Marc laughed. "Not so, sweet thing. A 'cattle call' is when they issue an open invitation to try out for the chorus and bit parts of a play through the trade papers. It's unbelievable how many starving actors there are in New York City. Why the line can stretch for blocks and the selection can take days."

"You'd help in the selection process?"

"Not directly. I have only minor creative control, but it's awesome to watch a play being built from the stage up, you might say. Wouldn't you like to stay for a while longer and be a part of it?"

Callie uncurled her legs, stretching them out in front of her, and leaned back on her palms. *Stay!* Was it possible for her to stay, even if only for a little while longer? "It's worth thinking about."

She reminded him of a skittish kitten, peeking cautiously around a doorframe into an unexplored room. "With your musical background, you've never participated in a play before?" he asked.

"In high school. I was to play the piano for the senior class production of *South Pacific*. Weren't we ambitious?" He raised his eyebrows higher. "Anyway, opening night I came down with the flu. Joan Elam—my archrival for choral pianist—stepped in and took over pretty as you please. I was so crushed that I've never gone near a stage again."

"Then your education is sadly lacking, my dear. You need to experience the smell of grease paint, the roar of the crowd!" He brandished his arms dramatically, laid his guitar on the bench, stood and bowed elaborately from his waist. "A lady should never slight her education."

Callie scrambled to her feet and curtsied, tugging on the seams of her jeans as if they were an Edwardian pinafore. "Perhaps you're right, m'lord." She went giddy with excitement. *Stay!* He caught her hand and kissed it. "I may never wash this hand again." She feigned a swoon and flapped her eyelashes.

Marc straightened slowly, capturing her eyes with his. A yellow-winged butterfly fluttered between them, a lazy graceful dancer pirouetting to an unheard cadence. Callie felt the pressure of her lungs against her ribcage, let out her breath in degrees, ensnared by the lure of green eyes. Marc stepped closer, pulling her hand within inches of his lips. The levity was gone. He wanted her in his arms. He knew she wanted to be in them. Reason told him not to take her. Tenderly, he turned her hand over and placed a kiss in her palm and closed her fist over it. "Think about it, Callie. Think about staying even for a little while longer."

Her skin glowed where his kiss lay, clutched in her hand. She wanted to stay. She wanted so much to stay.

"Mrs. Kaufman said I could come out here." The voice was Sol Rothstein's.

Self-consciously, Callie jerked her hand away and stepped to the edge of the flowerbeds, her cheeks hot.

Darkly, Marc turned to face his uncle who hadn't been in the house since the night of the infamous dinner party. Sol wore a charcoal-colored linen suit, a burgundy handkerchief poking from the top pocket, like an elegant afterthought. As usual he looked slick, composed, hawkish.

"You might have called first," Marc said.

"I have to call and make an appointment with my own nephew?" Sol's words said one thing, the tone of his voice quite another.

"When I'm working . . . yes."

Sol ignored him, swooping his gaze around the beauty of the garden. "That Japanese man has worked wonders. I'd say it's every bit as magnificent as when your mother tended it."

"If you want a tour of the grounds . . ."

"This isn't exactly a social call, Marc." Sol laid a thin leather attaché next to Marc's guitar on the bench. He snapped open the locks, and for the first time, Callie noted an air of smugness about him, the attitude an indulgent parent might take when dire warnings to a child were on the mark, the complacency that came with the words, "I told you so."

"If not a social call, then exactly what?"

From the briefcase Sol extracted a thick manila folder and held it out. His eyes became hard, cold, his voice steely. "This is filled with cancelled checks from your sister. All her finances routinely go through Rothstein's accounting department. Your father set it up that way years ago." He tossed the envelope down on the bench with a loud smack. "Since Rachael has been on her little 'vacation,' she's blown almost $200,000 at the casinos in Monte Carlo. Now, since you're her guardian angel, what are you going to do about it, Mr. Know-it-all?"

chapter 11

ONLY THE MOVEMENT OF THE MUSCLE in Marc's jaw signaled the immense control he was exerting over himself. Flabbergasted by Sol's announcement, Callie saw it twitch and was instinctively drawn to Marc's side.

"Elaborate, please."

Sol's eyes snapped, his smugness replaced by vindictive anger. "She's gambling away a fortune. I have her IOUs signed over to the biggest houses in Monte Carlo, cancelled checks . . . she's topped the limit on all her credit cards . . . in short, she's spending like a drunken sailor! At this rate, not even the Rothstein money can last. It's Daniel's inheritance you were so concerned about, wasn't it? Well, once his mother is finished, there'll be precious little for the boy to claim!"

Marc matched the glare in his uncle's eyes. "Thank you for bringing this to my attention, Sol. I'll handle it."

"What are you going to do about it?"

"All you need to know is that it will be handled. *What* I do about it is not your concern."

Sol sputtered, livid over Marc's dismissal of him. "I have a right—"

"She's my sister, and you have no rights." The iron edge in his voice cut off Sol's ire. Like dipping molten metal into water, Sol's malicious words sizzled and evaporated. Marc crossed the garden calmly, and opened the French doors. "Now that your message has been delivered, there's no reason for you to remain."

Sol jerked up his briefcase. "You've dug a fine hole for yourself this time, Marc. Your father was correct—a Christianized Jew isn't worthy to be a member of this family. He did the right thing by disowning you . . . too bad you've duped your sister into believing that *you* could be her salvation." Sol's chest heaved, his demeanor was challenging, threatening. When Marc refused to respond, he spat, "I'll leave the evidence with you," and stalked through the door, slamming it behind him.

Callie reached for Marc, herself stinging from Sol's vitriolic attack. "Oh, Marc! I'm so sorry. I can't believe he said those things to you. I can't believe Rachael would behave this way!"

"She left here hurt and wounded, running scared. She should never have run away." He appeared distracted as he spoke.

Of course, he was right. Callie felt doubly hit, by Rachael's actions and by her advice to Marc to allow Rachael to go in the first place.

Sensing her turmoil, Marc reached out and toyed with her hair. "Hey. No recriminations to yourself because I don't regret letting her go. Despite Uncle Sol's words, it's only money, Callie. What bothers me most is Rachael's inability to face herself . . . ask for help. She needed to discover that she couldn't buy her way out of her problems."

"It's an awful lot of money, Marc. What *are* you going to do?"

Resignation flirted with the corner of his mouth. Callie wanted to smooth it away. "I have her power of attorney, remember? I'm going to call our lawyers now and exercise it. Once I cut off the funds, she'll have no choice but to come home. I'll wire her the news with a one-way ticket to New York. With any luck, she'll be home in two days."

"She'll be out for blood."

"No doubt." He cocked his head to one side, adding, "I guess we'd better forget the fatted calf, hadn't we? She'll probably be more in the mood for 'head of brother.'"

His wry humor made Callie smile. "What can I do to help?"

"Your being here helps, Callie."

"What about Daniel?"

"Don't say anything to him about his mother coming home. I think Rachael and I'd better have it out before she sees her son." He walked from the sunshine of the garden, toward the cool interiors of the house. "I'll be spending most of the afternoon with lawyers. Would you work on the finale number? You know, the reprise of 'Shipwrecked Dreams' and the song we were composing for Caesar to sing as Paul's led off stage."

She remembered. The finale. Finis. The End. "I'll be in the music room if you need me."

Callie stood in the garden long minutes after Marc had left, her mind churning while the heavy scent of the myriad flowers made her lightheaded. Marc Raphael had the weight of the world on his shoulders. She was merely one more burden. His family need him. Rachael . . . Daniel . . .

Hope died inside her. Delusions. She'd been suffering delusions when she'd considered staying. She couldn't stay. She turned smartly on her heel, grinding the sole of her sandal against the flagstone and snuffing out her foolish fantasies.

Tension blanketed the house for two full days. Marc's wire to Rachael had brought a heated overseas phone call from his sister. He simply told her, "Your ticket's at Orly airport in Paris. Come home." She'd hung up in his ear.

Callie spent extra time with Daniel, reading to him, playing with him, hiding the late evening arrival of his mother from him. She slipped the covers over his small body and kissed his forehead. "Good night," she whispered.

"You're my bestest friend."

"You're my best friend, too."

"When Mama comes home, maybe you and Uncle Marc can write some more music together. I don't want you to go away, Callie."

His plea sliced through her. "We'll talk about it tomorrow." She needed to get away from him. It wasn't legal to care so much for him. She went down to the music room and waited with Marc for the chauffeur to return from the airport with Rachael. The clock on the wall ticked off the minutes in crawling increments, dragging the evening out with a plodding slowness that Callie thought would drive her mad.

Marc waited, playing an occasional piece on the piano, pacing, praying, preparing himself for his sister's wrath. She'd given him power of attorney as an act of trust, never expecting him to use it. She'd feel betrayed. Had he? Had he acted in her best interests? He thanked God that Callie was with him; her presence in the room gave him a sense of justification in his course of action. She'd stood in for his sister all these weeks with Daniel, loving him, giving so freely of herself to him, knowing there'd be nothing in return. He wanted to hold her against him, feel her in his arms, touch her face, and feel her arms around him. The room began to close in on him. How could time move so slowly?

A commotion in the sound lock caused both Marc and Callie to tense. With a violent heave, the inner door opened and Rachael Rothstein hurtled into the room. She was thinner even than Callie remembered. Her outfit, a throbbing blue Paris original, clung in folds of hand-embroidered silk. She looked expensive, almost garish in the newest fad make-up from the salons of France. She was white-lipped. She acknowledged no one, but crossed directly to Marc and shouted, "What do you think you're doing? How dare you summon me home like a naughty child! How dare you use legal power to manipulate me!"

Marc leaned lazily against the top of the piano. Callie recognized the stance, the same one he'd used when she'd come into his dressing room so many months before and flung her accusations at him about stealing her song. She saw tension inch between his shoulder blades. "Welcome home."

Rachael gritted, "I'm staying just long enough to get control of my estate from you. Then I'm going back to Europe."

"I think not." The calmness of his voice belied the steely set of his jaw.

Rachael exploded. "You're worse than Father! Pulling my strings like I'm some sort of a puppet. I won't stand for it! Do you hear me?" Her voice took on an edge of hysteria.

"Grow up, Rachael," Marc snapped, stopping her outburst. "Like it or not, you're here to stay for a while. I treat you like a child because you've acted like a child. Sol brought me your ledger sheets, Rachael. I know how much you've lost in Monte Carlo. Are those the actions of a calm, rational adult?"

She flushed. "It's my money and I can spend it however I please!"

"I could buy and sell you, Rachael. I've made that much money over the years. I know firsthand what money buys."

"Let me guess, Marc. 'It doesn't buy happiness.' Right?" She crossed her arms, tossing him a scornful look.

"I don't have to tell you that part. You already know it."

She whirled, turning her back to him. "Don't lecture me. . . ."

"It's Daniel's money, too. Or have you forgotten why you gave me legal control of your money in the first place." Marc cut her off. "Yes, Daniel's fine . . . ," he added; her face registered momentary shame at having forgotten the boy. "Thanks to Callie, who's stood in your stead all these weeks."

For the first time, Rachael faced Callie. "He's missed you, Rachael."

Marc intervened. "Did you know that Daniel started calling Callie, 'Mama'?"

Rachael paled. "T–That's not possible. . . ."

"Why not? She not only took care of him, she did a lot of

other things for him too. She helped him draw all those pictures we sent to you. She talked about you to him everyday . . . even went through the photo albums and put pictures of you up on his bulletin board . . . so he wouldn't forget you."

"I wrote him. . . ."

"You were gone, Rachael, and he needed you. He lost his grandfather and his mother. What does a four-year-old child know about letters postmarked from Europe?"

For a moment Rachael trembled as if teetering on the edge of a pit. Callie restrained herself from reaching out to her, turning tortured eyes toward Marc, who warned her to stay away. Rachael began to shiver, and her facial expression cracked like a porcelain mask. Her hands rose to cover her face, and she moaned, a wrenching sound. Just as her legs buckled, Marc caught her, pulling her to him, waiting while her anguish struggled to get out. "I feel like I'm going crazy. I–I'm so lonely. Help me, Marc. Please . . . please help me." Her voice was little more than a raspy whisper.

Carefully he sat her down on the sofa and crouched in front of her, grasping her hands in his, swallowing her delicate fingers in his. He forced her to look at him, pulling words from out of his soul. "Rachael . . . listen to me. I'm only your brother. Flesh and blood. *I* can't help you. But I know of Someone who can. Won't you please let me tell you about him?"

Rachael's eyes clung to Marc's, begging, pleading for a way out of her inner hell. Slowly, imperceptively, she nodded.

Callie floated around the bedroom that had been her home for the past three months. She touched the furniture, tenderly, as if by stroking it, she could memorize it, keep it with her somehow. Her opened suitcases yawned across the bed. She kept filling them, laying a dress one way, a pair of slacks another. Marc was still with his sister. Callie had left them, hours before while they talked. Rachael needed him.

She cleared the bathroom of her cosmetics, shampoos, and perfumes. A spritz of gardenia-scented cologne reminded her of the garden where she'd spent so many hours with Marc. "Dumb thing to do," she chided her reflection in the mirror. She ran her fingers over the gilt-edged faucets, trailing them carefully over the shiny spigots, recalling how the stagelights had glinted off the neck of Marc's guitar as his fingers coaxed sweet, sonorous notes from the instrument.

Hollow. She felt hollow inside. Empty. Like the night Kevin had died. Like the day the baby had left her. Her hand reached out to touch her face in the mirror. Her nails tapped against the cold glass, the thickness of the surface separating her from the warmth of her reflected skin. Twice in her lifetime she'd come so close to paradise. *Good-by, Marc* . . . Her life was ever a series of leavings. . . .

"I just put Rachael to bed. She's exhausted, but I think she's finally found some peace." Callie hadn't heard Marc come into the room, and she started at the sound of his voice. It didn't take him long to see the suitcases. Callie brushed past him, piling a handful of lingerie into the bag. "What's going on, Callie?"

"The play's essentially finished. I need to leave."

Shock, then fear swept through him. "I thought you might stay to see the production put together, like we discussed. Don't you want to be a part of that? There'll be publicity to do. The press will want to interview us, write about our collaboration." He felt desperate, like he was grabbing at straws. "Like it or not, we've created a major production."

"It's your play, Marc. I helped. But it was your vision, your dream. I'm honored to have been a part of it." Her hands twisted a delicate satin robe, betraying her turmoil. "I can't stay. Things are different now."

He willed her to turn and face him, but refused to touch her. If he did, he wasn't sure he could ever let go. "Rachael's home. What's different?"

She whirled, suddenly agitated. Why was he making this routine departure so difficult? "Daniel needs to be with his mother without me in the background. And they both need you desperately."

"What about what I need, Callie?"

She didn't respond. He had achieved the fulfillment of his dream with the completion of the musical, he certainly didn't need her cluttering up his life. "I've called a cab. It should be here shortly, and I don't want to keep it waiting."

Marc measured her with his eyes, leaned against the doorframe, shoved his hands into his pockets. He couldn't stop her. Nothing he could say would stop her. He tried not to imagine tomorrow morning without her beside him. The thought was so dark, so painful, that he glanced down at the floor. She was going. "You know what you remind me of, Callie?"

Only her hands, ceasing their constant folding motions gave evidence that she heard him. He said, "I went to the beach once, and I saw a man there with his little girl. She was about three years old, and it was obvious that she'd never seen the ocean before." His strange reminiscence made Callie look at him and his eyes pinioned her. "That child was overwhelmed at the sight of those waves rolling into the shore, but she was scared to death of them too. She kept running down to the edge of the water, yet the minute a wave threatened to touch her feet, she scampered back to the dry sand.

"Her father went into the water and called to her. She wanted to go. I could tell. She wanted so much to play with him in the surf. But she couldn't get over her fear. He coaxed and urged and pleaded. But she wouldn't go."

Callie's mouth felt dry, and her stomach knotted. She wanted to tear her eyes away from his, wanted to clamp her hands over her ears and scream, "Stop it! Stop it!" but she couldn't move.

"At the time, I thought it was funny. But looking back, I see now that it was also very sad. She never went into the water, Callie. She never enjoyed the pleasure of that beautiful ocean. And do you know what's the saddest part of all? It never once occurred to her that no matter how high the waves were . . . no matter if they knocked her down . . . her father was right there, ready to catch her. She wouldn't be hurt because her father's arms were inches away."

The silence in the room made the sound of Callie's own breathing a roar in her ears. Marc whispered, "*Shalom* . . ."

Callie watched him go, his oral picture haunting her

mind's eye. She shivered. Cold. She felt cold again. And empty . . . all poured out. She'd have to think of someplace to go. Where? Hadn't she wondered that very thing weeks before when Janette had called? Callie resumed her packing. She had forgotten to tell Marc that she loved him. An oversight. Now, she'd never get the chance again. The taxi would be coming soon. She rushed, almost in a panic, tossing clothing in wads into the suitcases. And, when the taxi arrived, she left the house without a backward glance, knowing that it and all its inhabitants were forever burned into her mind, etched like needlepoint into the fabric of her heart. A perverse night breeze spiraled the seductive scent of blossoms into the air.

"Where to, lady?"

"The airport," she told the cabbie. "And would you please roll up the window? For some reason, the air doesn't suit me tonight."

chapter 12

THE TWO ACTORS, SPOTLIGHTED on the darkened stage, moved in slow motion. The one, portraying Saul of Tarsus in chains, sang about eternal destiny, about unbridled hope with an eternal King. The other, playing Caesar, draped in royal purple and perched on a golden throne, sang counterpoint, "I am Caesar, king of kings. Who is this man that I should fear him?" The spotlights dimmed and then blinked off, leaving the stage in utter blackness. Suddenly, the audience in the theater erupted into applause, many standing, shouting.

Callie watched through the veil of mist in her eyes, as enthralled and captivated as the rest of the audience. She stood, clapping, until her hands stung, awed, touched, stunned by the impact of the performance she had just witnessed. She could hardly comprehend that she had helped create it, that her words, her music, had been brought to life so vividly by the performers who were taking curtain calls across the now-lighted stage.

Marc's genius had fueled her. Marc's vision had guided her, but she had worked with him, and together they had produced the music that had inflamed the hearts of the opening night audience. "Thank you, Lord," she whispered under her breath. The songs danced in her head while she made her way through the aisles clogged with the departing audience. When she heard them saying, "Stunning," "Magnificent," "I felt like I was in church," she smiled inwardly.

She imagined the bedlam backstage. Marc would be with the cast. There would be a party, press people, critics. By morning, all New York would know that a smash hit was appearing off-Broadway. Callie was satisfied. Marc deserved it. She tugged her thin evening wrap tightly around her shoulders as she stepped into the moist, spring night, breathing in the damp April air along with the smells of the city.

Exhaust fumes merged with sounds and lights to paint a kaleidoscope of impressions for her. This city was like no other, anywhere. Nostalgia dogged her as she remembered all the years she'd spent in New York. So many memories . . . Callie hailed a cab, resisting the swing to melancholia, content to inch along in the congested traffic during the long ride to her hotel suite through concrete corridors, banked by soaring skyscrapers.

She'd been gone eight months—eight months from when she'd fled Marc's home, Marc's life. In some ways, it seemed like a lifetime; in others, it seemed like only yesterday. Maybe it was the time of year, for it was April when she'd come to begin work on the musical. No matter. Tonight her self-imposed exile was over. She'd returned to the city that never sleeps to attend the opening of the play and to . . . to what? *Marc.* The thought of him kept sneaking up on her mind, springing out to startle her when she least expected it. Somehow the cab stalled in traffic in front of Rothstein's. She gazed at the impervious black marble facade, lighted indirectly by track spots from generous display windows. The newest in spring fashions filled the windows, on mannequins, posed for a lifetime of insulated protection. She'd been like a mannequin once, sheltered and protected. But no more. Life had taught her to depend on God, not others, for her safety.

At her hotel, she paid the driver and went directly to her room, ignoring the open stares of men as she swept through the lobby in her muted rainbow-hued gown in iridescent taffeta. Her room was quiet. She tossed off the coat, kicked off her satin-strapped sandal heels, and settled in a chair to wait. Rachael would be coming soon. This visit was the price Rachael had extracted for getting Callie a ticket for the opening night performance. "Callie! Where are you?" Rachael had gasped the week before when Callie had phoned. "Where have you been all this time? Why did you leave so suddenly? Where did you go? When can I see you?"

"I'm at the airport, and please don't ask me a lot of questions, Rachael. I'll tell you everything very soon. But believe me, I'm fine. In fact, I'm better than I've been in years. I want to see the play. I know it's opening next week."

"Marc can—"

Callie cut her off. "Don't tell Marc. Please, Rachael. I–I'm not ready to see him yet. And he doesn't need the distraction just before the opening. Will you help me?" And Rachael Rothstein had. She'd sent the ticket, kept Callie's secret, but had demanded to come visit her after the performance. When the knock came on her door, Callie rose to let Rachael in.

Rachael looked so lovely that for a moment Callie didn't recognize her. Gone were the haggard, gaunt face, the listless eyes, the thin figure. She looked radiant, beautiful, lit by an inner beauty that seeped from her very pores. "Oh, Rachael!" The two women embraced, then backed off, self-consciously, absorbing one another with their eyes. "You look wonderful!" Callie meant it.

"Thank you. So do you, Callie. Do you have any idea how much we've missed you?" Rachael stripped off her evening coat to reveal a gown of black beaded voile laced with threads of gold.

Callie heard her use of the plural "we." "How's Daniel?"

"He had a birthday last February. Now that he's five, he knows everything. His mother's stupidity is a constant source of embarrassment to him. I took your advice, Callie. He's in school now and has so many little friends I can't keep their names straight." They laughed together. Rachael sobered and added, "He missed you terribly when you left."

Callie stared down at her champagne-hued nails. "I'm sorry I left without telling him good-by. I didn't know how to say it. I told myself that you would understand. Do you?"

"Of course, I know exactly why you left, Callie. I know you wanted to give Daniel and me a chance to become mother and son again. I know you guessed how much we both needed Marc."

Callie exhaled, pensive, but satisfied. She eyed Rachael, surveyed her radiant face from beneath puckered brows.

There was something else going on. . . . It came to Callie in a flash. "Rachael Rothstein! You're in love!"

"It shows?"

Like a candle in the night. Who is he?"

Rachael's voice assumed soft shyness. "His name is Benjamin Elbow. He's a Messianic Jew . . . like me. And I love him so much, Callie. It's like starting life all over again."

Callie tapped her bare foot impatiently on the carpet. "Spill it," she demanded.

"After that night I returned from Europe—" Rachael shuddered involuntarily. "When Marc talked to me about Jesus Christ, I thought, 'Could it be that simple?' I decided to find out for myself. I started reading the New Testament, and I began attending a group meeting with other born-again Jews. Ben is the leader, the shepherd, you might say. Oh, Callie he's so wonderful! So filled with purpose and the Spirit of God. He's helped me understand what it is to be Jewish. Not just the ritualistic, nationalistic thing my family was, but a completed Jew . . . a person set apart for God Himself."

She rotated her shoulders in a gesture of self-consciousness. "Ben loves me . . . and Daniel too . . . I can't wait for you to meet him." Her eyes clouded and she reached for Callie's arm. "You will be staying, won't you? You must come to the house. Please, for Daniel's sake."

Callie turned aside, paced to the window, hugging her arms to herself. She wanted to see Daniel again. She wanted to meet Ben Elbow. But most of all, she wanted to see Marc. Would he want to see her. "I'm scared, Rachael. I've missed Marc so much that it actually aches. I saw his face in every dream, heard his voice in lines of songs. Not a day passed that he wasn't in my mind and heart. But I left so suddenly. And so completely. How is he? What's he doing?"

"He's fine." Rachael's tone was guarded.

Callie asked the question that haunted her most of all. "Does he have . . . is there anyone else in his life? Please tell me the truth, Rachael."

"There's never been anyone else, Callie. He's worked like a madman since you left. The play became his whole life. He did some touring and his record company put 'Gifted' out as a single. It's at the top of the Christian music charts."

Callie sagged, weak with relief. Marc had no other woman. She barely heard the news about the song. "What will he do now that the play's over."

"He's staying at the house right now but is planning to return to Nashville and his concert tours in a few days."

Callie watched the traffic crawl on the street below her. Bright headlights inched behind vivid red tailights. Moisture condensed on the window pane. Her breath caused the glass to cloud. "He—he said once that I was afraid of commitment . . . and he was right. But do you know what's even worse than the fear? It's not having anyone to be committed to." Callie seemed almost to be speaking to herself.

Rachael stood next to her, and together they gazed out over the city sprinkled with neon glitter. "Love takes chances, Callie. Once—a long time ago—I told you that something needed settling between you and my brother."

Callie remembered. "You spent four months of your lives together writing that musical and you never settled it. It's about time you did. You know where he is, you know you to get there. Go to him. For both your sakes, go to him."

Callie came to the garden in the early morning hours, when a thin layer of dew hung on shrubs and delicate bursts of pastel flowers, knowing instinctively Marc would be there. He wore a cream-colored knit sweater, faded jeans, and suede boots. His guitar lay propped next to him on the bench. She watched him for a time, feasting her eyes on his profile, the strong line of his jaw, the thick chestnut hair and patrician nose. *I love him . . .*, she confessed silently. But she'd known that for months. In all honesty, almost from the first time he'd looked into her eyes, invited her to join him for dinner in Canada. He'd said, "Come with me." And she had. Down every step of the long road to this moment. *Let me say the right things, Lord. Let me be a part of his life again.*

The garden had been reborn, resplendent with blossoms of pink and fuschia, lavender and white. It sported legions of lilies and bushes laden with buds brushed by leafy fingers of ferns, more delicate than lace. Slanting rays from the morning sun spilled over the flagstones, dappling the flowerbeds with small circles of lemon-colored light. The rich, loamy smell of earth assailed her. She shoved her hands into the pockets of her nylon jacket and walked into a large puddle of light. Marc looked up at the sound of her footfall. Her heart stuck in her throat.

If he was surprised to see her, he didn't show it. He rose from his seated position and faced her. "Hello, Callie." Whatever she'd expected, it wasn't this, a gentle greeting, as if she'd merely slipped away for a few moments instead of almost eight months.

"Hello yourself."

Marc was stunned to see her, but he held his shock in an iron grip. What if she were a mirage? Only God knew how often he'd imagined she'd appear like this one day before him. Marc appraised her, drinking in the red-blond curls that softly framed her face, her liquid brown eyes, the sooty fringe of her lashes. He loved her. God help him, he loved her still. But she'd been away so long. Why had she returned now? "The play opened last night. We've got a hit on our hands."

"I heard. Is this how you celebrate? Alone?"

"I left the cast party at midnight. I was all partied out."

She scraped the heel of her boot on the stone, as if to gather the sunlight closer to her body. "Congratulations, Marc. You deserve every good thing God can give you."

"Where have you been, Callie?" His question was so soft, she almost didn't catch it. "Have you any idea how I looked for you? Nothing. For eight months, nothing."

She wanted to hide from the hurt she read in his green eyes. "I had to work some things out for myself, Marc."

"I checked with the Hansons. All Farrell would tell me was that you were safe."

She licked her lips nervously. "Don't hold it against them, please. They kept my secret because I begged them to."

"Where were you?"

"You'll laugh."

"Amuse me."

"Israel."

Marc laughed. "Israel? Callie, I'm a Jew and I've never been to Israel."

"You should go. It's a very unique country." She paced to the edge of a flowerbed and absently fingered a velvet pink flower. "Everybody's either in the army or fixing to join it. You Jews are a fierce and proud people, Marc."

"We Jews are a resilient people, Callie." She heard a hidden meaning in his words and wondered, *How resilient?* He asked, "How did you end up in Israel?"

"Well, there I stood in the airport with my bags packed. All dressed up with no place to go, you might say. I didn't want to return to Michigan. I couldn't stay here." She pulled petals from the hapless blossom. "I looked up and saw this poster on the terminal wall. It said, 'Come visit the Holy Land.'" She shrugged. "So I did."

He raked fingers through his hair, trailing his hand to the nape of his neck, shaking his head in disbelief. "For eights months? You were a tourist in Israel for eights months?"

"Yes . . . at first. It took a couple of weeks to get my passport, but once I got there I did everything I could as a tourist. Israel is very beautiful. Not like this country at all. But wild and ancient. Mostly sand and rocks and hills. It turns green very quickly, when the rains come. Then turns brown just as fast. The green is brief and bright. Emerald green." *I'm babbling,* she told herself. She gestured around the garden. "It will never look like this.

"But Jerusalem! Oh, Marc, Jerusalem is—" She groped for words to describe it, her eyes shining. "—the spiritual center of the universe. Jews, Moslems, Christians . . . they're all there in the 'City of God.' It's surrounded by hills, like God's cupping it in his hand." She curved her palm to illustrate her point. "The City of Zion. Most of the religious history of the world happened there. I started with the Wailing Wall in the Old City."

"The place where all the Jews migrate to mourn their past . . . yes, I know. They weep for yesterday—for themselves, really."

"Old people mostly. They just stood before it and cried." She shook off the memory. "I also walked the Via Dolorosa—where Christ dragged his cross for his crucifixion. And I went to Bethlehem too."

"But for so long. How could you have stayed there so long?"

She paced to the far side of the garden, turned to face him, and pushed down the lump forming in her throat. "I lived on a *kibbutz.* Farrell helped me, through some contacts he had over there. I was a volunteer worker for a collective farm in the North. I woke every morning and looked out to Mt. Hermon. It's Israel's greatest landmark, you know. From Hermon to the Jordan, God gave the land to the Israelites. I don't think anyone will ever take it back from them either."

Marc folded his arms, never taking his eyes from her face. "*Kibbutz* living can be dangerous."

"There were bomb shelters on the grounds, but we didn't have to use them. I worked in the children's houses most of the time." She held up her palms. "Dishpan hands." She smiled weakly.

Marc's heart thudded. "You could have been hurt."

"My best friend was a *nachal* girl—a woman in the army. She taught me a lot about survival." A robin fluttered in a nearby tree, and Callie absently plucked another flower, spinning the stem in her fingers. "I worked hard, but it was good for me. On my days off, I saw every bit of the country that I could."

Marc rubbed the back of his neck in an effort to ease the tension crouched along his muscles. Callie continued, "I saw the Sea of Galilee and the River Jordan, and I took one very long sidetrip into the Sinai." Her eyes bore into his. "The Sinai isn't beautiful at all, Marc. It's hot and brutal. Even the stones are unfriendly. Strange that God would chose such a wilderness to talk to his people."

"Well, we didn't listen so well in Eden. Maybe he thought there'd be fewer distractions in a desert."

"A person is alone out there, Marc. Utterly alone." Her voice grew breathy, quavering with intensity for the things she wanted to share with him. "And if she's very blessed, God talks to her out there. Even now."

Marc reached out and tugged on a curl, allowing himself to touch her for the first time. The gesture of familiarity almost unraveled her. "What did he say to you, Callie?"

"Marc . . . I've spent the last four years of my life mourning over the things I've lost. Always looking back, always dwelling on the past. I was a lot like all those people I met in Israel. They never see tomorrow. They're forever focused on their heritage, forever looking behind them on what *was* instead of what *is*."

"It's a common failing of Zionism."

"I never once considered the wonderful new places God was leading me and the gifts he was giving me now."

"Such as?"

She traced her tongue over dry lips, desperate to control the fearful hammering of her heart, the trembling of her hands. "Such as the opportunity to write the musical. And

Rachael and Daniel. And you." Her voice dropped to a hoarse whisper. She feared her heart might crash through the wall of her breast.

"What are you going to do about it, Callie?"

He was making her go all the way to him, total surrender . . . and he wouldn't make it easier for her. Once she revealed her heart to him, he could shut her off, laugh at her, toss her out. But that was the chance she had to take, the price Marc Raphael was extracting. Callie felt as if ocean waves were about to swamp her. *Help me, Lord.* She tipped her chin upwards, let the light of mischief danced in her thoughts. She cleared her throat. "Mr. Raphael, once I asked you to make love to me and you turned me down flat."

"I meant to mention the streak of insanity that sometimes emerges in the family line."

"Given that rejection, you give me no recourse except to ask you to marry me."

For a few heart-thudding moments, he didn't speak. Then she saw a smile spark in his eyes and drift lazily down to tilt the corner of his delicious mouth. "Are you trying to make an honest man of me, Ms. O'Ryan?"

"Someone has to. It's about time you got off the bachelor roles and left all those poor, tormented teenage girls in peace."

"Tormented, Callie? Let me tell you about tormenting." He caught her in his arms so quickly that Callie scarcely had time to catch her breath. She only knew she was pressed hard against him, and he was kissing her, melting her, absorbing her, filling her with demands and promises. She clung to him, tasting, wanting, giving. His mouth taunted, greedily taking what he had so long desired. He caressed her face, trailed kisses down her cheek, across her taut throat to the throbbing pulse in its hollow. If she had not been leaning against him, her legs could not have held her.

She tangled her fingers through his hair. "I love you, Marc. I love you so much."

He stopped his assault on her senses long enough to demand, "This had better be the shortest engagement in human history, Callie. I'm out of patience."

"Just give me enough time to gather a bridal bouquet."

"Well, if that's all you want. . . ." He pushed away slightly, holding her arm, refusing to let go of her, and bent to pluck a flower. He laid it in her cupped hands and then stood stunned by the impact of her response. "I–I didn't mean to make you cry. . . ."

Callie stared at the cradled blossom, unable to utter a sound.

"It's only a rosebud." His eyes scanned barren, fresh planted rows of rose bushes. "In fact, it looks like the first rose of the season. I'm surprised it's even blooming this early in the year. Are you all right?"

She nodded and managed to say, thickly, "It's just that yellow roses have always been my favorites."

"I didn't know that."

"Only one Person knows."

His brow puckered at her enigmatic response. "If you like yellow roses Callie, my love, you shall have a room full of them on our wedding day. Consider it a gift from your bridegroom."

She raised on tiptoe, surrendering herself to his lips, the

flower forgotten. As her arms encircled his neck, the rose caught between them, its delicate petals bending and crushing, releasing its sweet, heady perfume to mingle with their kiss.

ABOUT THE AUTHOR

A prolific author, LURLENE MCDANIEL has written eighteen books for *School Book Fairs Willowisp Press*. This is her fourth inspirational romance for Serenade Books, following *Eternal Flame, Hold Fast the Dream,* and *Love's Full Circle,* a book that has evoked much favorable reader response.

McDaniel is also a writing instructor, a public relations specialist, and a columnist for *The Christian Writer*.

She lives in Florida with her family, is active in her local church, and participates in an Artist Support Group that has dedicated itself to redeeming the arts for the kingdom of God.

A Letter to Our Readers

Dear Reader:

Welcome to Serenade Books—a series designed to bring you beautiful love stories in the world of inspirational romance. They will uplift you, encourage you, and provide hours of wholesome entertainment, so thousands of readers have testified. That we might better contribute to your reading enjoyment, we would appreciate your taking a few minutes to respond to the following questions and return to:

> Lois Taylor
> Serenade Books
> The Zondervan Publishing House
> 1415 Lake Drive, S.E.
> Grand Rapids, Michigan 49506

1. Did you enjoy reading *A Gift of Love*?

   ☐ Very much. I would like to see more books by this author!
   ☐ Moderately
   ☐ I would have enjoyed it more if ______________________

2. Where did you purchase this book? ______________________

3. What influenced your decision to purchase this book?

   ☐ Cover ☐ Back cover copy
   ☐ Title ☐ Friends
   ☐ Publicity ☐ Other ______________

4. Please rate the following elements from 1 (poor) to 10 (superior).

☐ Heroine
☐ Hero
☐ Setting
☐ Plot
☐ Inspirational theme
☐ Secondary characters

5. What are some inspirational themes you would like to see treated in future books?

____

____

6. Please indicate your age range:

☐ Under 18
☐ 18–24
☐ 25–34
☐ 35–45
☐ 46–55
☐ Over 55